By Megan Bryce

The Fashionista Falls...
Boring Is The New Black

A Temporary Engagement
Some Like It Charming
Some Like It Ruthless
Some Like It Perfect
Some Like It Hopeless

The Reluctant Bride Collection
To Catch A Spinster
To Tame A Dragon
To Wed The Widow
To Tempt the Saint

BORING
is the new
BLACK

The fashionista falls...

Megan Bryce

Boring Is The New Black
The Fashionista Falls... Book One
Copyright © 2016 by Megan Bryce
All rights reserved.

ISBN: 1532763379
ISBN-13: 978-1532763373

meganbrycebooks@gmail.com

If you would like to be notified when a new title becomes available, sign up at **meganbryce.com**

To my husband–
Yes, I've already tried turning it off and on again. Fix it.

And to Lynn–
Because without her, and one fun weekend in Vegas, this series would never have been born.

One

There was no busier week for a fashion designer than the second week in February.

Designers, models, celebrities, and industry professionals of every variety swarmed New York, and it was no time for Nicole Bissette to be dawdling in a coffeehouse, *sitting down* even, when there were outfits to final check, lighting and music to run through. Problems to fix, fires to put out.

Except even during the busiest week of the year, there was time for very good friends. Best friends who'd dropped everything to come and lend moral support.

But only five minutes.

Gia unwound the pink, orange, and brown scarf from around her neck and said, "You only scheduled in five minutes for us to talk you off the ledge?"

She licked the whipped cream from off the top of her hot cocoa, and Nicole hadn't even known they served whipped cream. In New York. During fashion week.

"I can maybe push it to ten."

Victoria crossed her high-heeled black boots, smoothed her black ankle-length pencil skirt, blew on her extra-hot black coffee, and said, "We can do it in five."

"Thank you. Thank you for coming so quickly."

"What else are we going to do when our friend puts on her very first runway?" Gia squealed under her breath, her excitement uncontainable. "The friend who got us front-row seats for tomorrow!"

Nicole thought of everyone who was going to be sitting front row tomorrow. Critiquing her creations, comparing her to those who came before her that week.

Last year.

Twenty years ago.

She said, "I think I'm going to vomit."

"No, you're not." Victoria assessed the green pallor of her friend's skin. "Well, maybe you are. But then you are going to brush your teeth and redo your makeup, and have the best show New York has ever seen."

"It won't matter. How good it is. They'll say it's just because of *her*. And then if it's not good, it will be all my fault."

Gia puckered her eyebrows. "No one will say that."

Victoria nodded. "Yes, they will. So, what?"

Gia glared. "Victoria!"

"They will say it. And they will think it. And there's nothing she can do about that except give up."

Nicole put her head in her hands.

Gia rustled around in her large handbag. "Who cares if her mother is *Nikita*! She's her own person."

Nicole had never been her own person. She'd always been the daughter of. Always been the lesser of.

Her mother had been the trailblazer. Coming to America and first rocking the modeling world and then transitioning into a fierce fashion designer.

She'd fought her way to the top, tooth and nail. She'd worked for everything she had.

Nicole had never had the opportunity.

Doors opened without her having to even knock. Room was found without her having to even ask.

She was the daughter of fame. She was the daughter of money and power.

Everything had been handed to her since the day of her birth, and she couldn't undo her connections.

Victoria understood. Victoria Edwards knew what it meant to be the daughter of someone. Knew how to live in the shadows of the mighty. Knew how to fight for her own sun.

Gia finally found what she was looking for, pulling out a little bag of brightly colored candy and popping it open loudly before pushing it over.

"Take two handfuls and call me in the morning."

Nicole lifted her head to stare incredulously at her friend. "You have candy in your bag?"

"Of course I do. Candy makes everything better. Or to be more specific, sugar. Sugar makes everything better."

Victoria drawled, "We wouldn't know. Sugar is not something we're overly familiar with."

Gia eyed Victoria's coffee and her size two skirt. "I know. I'm so sorry."

Nicole pushed the candy away and sipped her small non-fat sugar-free vanilla extra foam cappuccino.

"Why did I become a designer? I'll always be her daughter, I'll always be competing against her. I should have gone into banking."

Victoria choked back her laughter. "You know this is your world. You're just afraid you will come up short. And you will. Accept it, embrace it. And look forward to that day when you won't. Now *that* will be an accomplishment."

Gia glared again. "Has anyone ever told you, Victoria, that you could use a little sugar?"

"Has anyone ever told you, Gia, that you could use a little less?"

This fight was as old as they were, though the sugar description was new. Since Giada Abelli had entered their exclusive boarding school on a scholarship, Victoria had been trying to get her to toughen up.

And Gia had been trying to get Victoria to soften up.

Gia picked up the bag of candy and waved it at Victoria.

"There are two kinds of people in this world: gummy bears and Sour Patch Kids. I think we know which of us is which. And I think we know which one is liked better."

She popped a gummy bear into her mouth and chewed ecstatically.

Victoria was unimpressed. "Who cares about being liked?"

"I do. And Nicole does."

Victoria made a face. "No, she cares about being respected. There's a difference."

Nicole watched the little bag of candy swing in her friend's hand. "If Gia's a gummy bear and Victoria's a Sour Patch Kid, what am I?"

Gia swallowed. "You're a Sour Patch Kid."

Victoria sipped. "You're a gummy bear."

Gia guffawed at Victoria. "She never smiles! How is that a gummy bear?"

Nicole never smiled because when she did she looked like her mother twenty years ago and no one let her forget it.

Straight brown hair that was somehow exotic on her mother and plain on Nicole.

Brown eyes that laughed and jabbed on her mother and were guarded on Nicole.

Full lips that were welcoming and sensual on both of

them. When they smiled.

"That's just my thing," Nicole said.

Gia popped another gummy bear into her mouth. "You're proving my point."

Victoria said, "I don't know what smiling has to do with it. I smile."

Victoria smiled then– a large beauty queen smile. Her straight white teeth gleaming, her brown eyes sparkling. Her long brown hair full and sexy.

And if anybody was stupid enough to fall for that smile, they would realize their mistake fairly quickly.

Gia nodded. "Okay. You're right. You smile an awful lot and no one would confuse you with a gummy bear."

"Thank you," Victoria said and meant it.

Gia rolled her eyes. "But Nicole is still not a gummy bear."

Nicole didn't want to be a gummy bear. But she didn't want to be a Sour Patch Kid, either.

Because no matter how much she looked like her mother, and no matter that she'd modeled like her mother, and now designed like her mother, Nicole wasn't her.

Wasn't like her mother *at all*.

Or much at all.

Her mother was a Sour Patch Kid and proud of it, just like Victoria.

Or something even more pucker-worthy than that.

Maybe a Hot Tamale or an Atomic Fireball, except that implied a sweetness under the spicy and right about there the whole candy reference fell apart.

Her mother was a firework. Pretty to look at, hot to the touch, just waiting to blow your arm off.

Nicole had been happy to get away from her to go to boarding school. Had been relieved to be on her own, even if it was amidst a pack of teenage girls.

Teenage girls were nothing compared to her mother.

Nicole had even been surprised to find a friend in Victoria.

Another refugee from a gilded, war-torn life and they'd joked about what a vacation school was from real life.

But not everyone had been prepared for the claws. Not everyone had been hardened in the crucible of drugs, sex, and money.

Some girls came from happy homes, with loving mothers and fathers. Family dinners.

Some girls were too nice for an all-girls boarding school.

One girl had been unprepared for a pack of hyenas to circle around, laughing and pulling at her too-frizzy hair, poking at the baby fat spilling over her skirt.

Gia had sucked in her stomach and patted her thick, brown hair, and said like she was repeating what some kindhearted grandmother had told her years ago, "A bird loves her nest."

The blond hair, blue-eyed ringleader had chirped a laugh. "Nest is right. Let's get some eggs, girls!"

Victoria, never afraid, had stepped inside the circle, pushing girls away left and right and smiling that smile. "Back off, Barbie."

Nicole had watched, nervous and wide-eyed.

Was she supposed to follow her friend? Into the middle of that circle?

But with someone fierce beside her, Gia had stuck her hands in her hair, shaking it wildly and saying, "Every bird must hatch its own eggs!"

The blond barbie had backed away, tossing her hair and smiling-slash-sneering, and when everyone was gone except the three of them, Victoria had turned to Gia.

"That made no sense."

"That was my plan."

And that had been it. It had been the three of them through three years of boarding school and then four more years of college.

Gia, her hair still corkscrew curly, wild and untamed, studied a bear between her fingers.

"Maybe there are three kinds of people: gummy bears, Sour Patch Kids, and Sour Patch Kids who think they're gummy bears." She waved the bear around. "Maybe even more than that. Gummy bears who wish they were Sour Patch Kids, Sour Patch Kids who wish they were gummy bear, Sour Patch Kids who love being a Sour Patch Kid, and Sour Patch Kids who don't know they're Sour Patch Kids, gummy bears who–"

Victoria closed her eyes. "Please, stop."

Nicole eyed the bag. "Maybe sugar does make everything better. Gia is pretty happy."

Really, she was the only one. Victoria was too intense to endure a mild feeling like happiness and Nicole was. . .just not.

Maybe it was the lack of sugar.

Victoria stood abruptly, ripping the bag from Gia's fingers and marching over to the nearest garbage can.

Gia cried out, "*Hey*," as Victoria threw it in and then marched back to the table.

"Nicole is already stressed and exhausted. She doesn't need to start eating candy on top of it and have to add more hours in at the gym."

Nicole nodded gratefully. "You're right. And it's already been eleven minutes. I have to get back anyway."

Gia shook her head. "Something is wrong with you two. Seriously."

Victoria checked her phone, eleven minutes as long as she could be away from her business as well.

"It's nothing a great runway won't fix."

Nicole stood, gathering her coat and shrugging into it. "We'll see. Anything better than 'It made me want to slit my throat' and I suppose I'll survive."

Gia said, like she wished she could believe it, "Your mother wouldn't say that about *your* runway."

Nicole and Victoria just looked at her and then at each other.

Victoria drawled, "It must be nice to grow up with loving family members who insist on not preparing you for real life."

Nicole nodded. "Must be. Now, was I talked off the ledge? I can't tell."

Gia stood, hugging her hard. "Enjoy your show. This first time will only come once."

Victoria shook her head in disgust. "Enjoy the memories. Now, go back to work and get it done."

There was *so much* work to be done and Nicole waved as she headed to the door, pausing before opening it to the cold and the wind, and then hurrying out before she could change her mind.

Through the glass window, Gia was waving at her enthusiastically and Victoria was smiling her beauty queen smile.

They'd be front and center tomorrow, along with half of New York.

And the other half would read about it the next day.

Nicole hugged her coffee cup to her chest, happy to be invisible right now in the crush of the crowded sidewalk.

Wishing she could be invisible tomorrow, too, and wondering what madness had come over her to think she could do a runway when her last name was Bissette.

Two

Flynn Redmond frequently wondered how he'd ever come to work for a fashion designer. For Nicole Bissette.

A celebrity, a debutante. The daughter of a supermodel.

But six months ago, she'd been hiring an IT Specialist (at an entry level salary), and that's what he was.

And what man wouldn't think that working with celebrities and models, who frequently pranced around in an undressed state, wouldn't be the most badass job ever?

He'd been wrong.

And he'd been surprised to learn that a lot of them were really young. They were overworked and underpaid. They were bored.

They were photoshopped, almost always.

And he could have done the photoshop but that wasn't his job.

His job was to keep the computers working. And the tablets. And the printers.

To update software and keep the website running.

To keep the wifi connected, the phones working.

No one wanted to be in a room full of bored models whose phones weren't working.

"It doesn't work. *Make it work*."

Flynn held out his hand for the phone, keeping his eyes off the semi-nude model sitting in her chair getting her hair and makeup done not because he was a decent human being but because it had only taken a few months before the allure of so much flesh had become completely and utterly normal.

In quiet moments, Flynn shook his fist at a cruel and unjust god. He couldn't look without knowing what parts had been nicked and tucked, photoshopped and retouched, and it was a sad day indeed when a healthy, red-blooded man got tired of nudity.

He said, "Have you tried turning it off and on again?"

She wasn't listening to him and didn't answer and wouldn't have got the reference anyway, and he turned the phone off and on again.

He handed it back to her with a "voila" and went back to watch from the sidelines.

He was just here to make sure everything was plugged in and turned on. If something wasn't working– and for some reason even when it wasn't technology related they called for him– it was his job to fix it.

This is what he'd spent four years in school for. What he'd accrued thousands and thousands of dollars of debt for.

A job full of naked women requiring him to drop whatever he was doing at any hour because no one in the fashion world had ever heard of nine to five.

Regular hours. He'd love regular hours.

Before Flynn had made it back to his watching position, he'd taped down a few cords that had worked their way loose, turned off and on two more phones, and changed the batteries in a microphone.

He was a regular jack-of-all-trades. A MacGyver!

Averting disaster and potentially explosive situations with duct tape and his thumb!

And no one here would get that reference either.

He stopped dead in his tracks when he saw Nicole Bissette huddled beside the AV cart, her knees tucked under chin and her eyes staring vacantly at a spot on the floor.

And then he shook his head in unsurprised resignation. The stress, the drugs, and he had no doubt the hunger, got to them all eventually.

To be fair, Nicole had never flown off the handle around him, and despite knowing that she had modeled for a few short years, he couldn't see her ever doing it.

Couldn't see her strutting around and being watched.

She was the watcher, staring at those around her as if she could see every ugly thought in their head.

And Flynn wondered again how he'd ever been hired. And why he hadn't been fired yet.

He inched closer. "Are you okay?"

Her eyes flicked to his, then back down. She wiggled her fingers at him to go away.

He said, "Should I get someone...else?"

She shook her head.

"Are you on something?"

Oh, no. She was tripping, right here. Geeking out, going to start screaming and ripping her hair out in chunks.

She whispered, "No. I just saw..."

Bugs burrowing out of her skin? A demon laughing at her from the back of someone else's head?

Flynn told himself once again that he really needed to find another job. Maybe in a library. He could like working in a library.

"My mother."

Flynn abruptly stopped worrying about her being on

drugs. She *had* seen a demon smiling.

Nikita was known the fashion world over, though Flynn had luckily never had the opportunity to meet her in person.

There were perks to working in the utility closet sometimes. It was easy to hide.

He looked behind him, letting out a breath when Nikita wasn't there.

Nicole was watching him when he turned back around and she jerked her head toward the crowd. "Out there."

"You want me to pull up the video?"

She nodded her head, then shook her head, then nodded her head.

He waited for her to make a decision and then. . .just pulled it up.

He flipped through the cameras until he found who he was looking for. "Here you go."

Nicole didn't get up, just said, "Is she smiling?"

"Yes."

"The 'How did I ever get talked in to coming to this fiasco' smile or the 'Let's see what kind of disaster this is going to turn out to be' smile?"

"Uh, I don't know." He squinted at the screen, then shrugged. "Now she's laughing."

Nicole closed her eyes. "Oh, God. Dear God."

His walkie-talkie crackled and a frantic female voice said, "Has anyone seen Nicole? Nicole? We need you at the front."

He said like she hadn't heard, when anyone within a ten foot radius could have, "They need you. They're starting."

She held her hand out to him to be helped up and Flynn suddenly remembered this woman was his boss.

He grabbed her hand and pulled gently.

She nodded her thanks, smoothed her pantsuit, and then glanced at the screen.

She took in the filled seats, her mother front row and center, and said, "That's the 'She'd better not embarrass me' smile. And the 'I'll skewer her if she does' laugh."

Flynn watched Nicole walk away, looking put together and like she hadn't just been huddling in a corner, and he heard her mutter, "I really should have become a banker."

Three

Hair. Makeup. Top. Bottom. Shoes.
Hair. Makeup. Top. Bottom. Shoes.

Model after model, Nicole checked one last time to make sure everything was perfect. Or as perfect as she could get it in these final moments.

The runway was a performance– the clothes the lines, the girls the actors.

This was art.

Colors and patterns and shapes that would be stocked by retailers in the fall and winter season, if she was lucky.

The music gave its cue, the lighting changed its color, and Nicole nodded because she couldn't say it.

Go.

The first girl went out and Nicole was too busy to check the TV for the audiences reaction. She'd watch the video after.

She was too busy to remember her own modeling days, not that she'd been any good at it. Too guarded and stiff. Too uncomfortable with everyone looking at her and comparing her.

The comparison could only be unfavorable.

She liked being behind the curtain. She liked being the one making decisions and bringing her visions to fruition. She liked being in charge.

And she was too busy to worry much about having to come out from behind the curtain to receive her applause.

Please let there be applause.

But the last girl was walking down the runway and the girls were lined up for their finale walk and Nicole was getting checked and finalized. Brushed and patted and manhandled. And she remembered another reason why she'd hated being a model.

Didn't like to be touched.

The final outfit of the collection was hers– a pale vanilla pantsuit topped with a chocolate peacoat– and when the last girl passed her, she waited three extra beats, then followed.

Nicole lifted her head, staring fiercely at nothing and strutting out behind her girls.

She moved with quick staccato steps, concentrating on staying far enough behind the last girl and ignoring the crowd.

She knew when she passed Gia and Victoria because they both stood, and Gia's rambunctious clapping almost made Nicole smile.

She knew when she passed Nikita from the dip in temperature.

The applause grew louder as she turned the first corner, a few more members of the audience stood up as she swept by them, and then suddenly everyone realized.

That *this* was Nicole Bissette. Walking in one of her own outfits.

And then a roar of applause. An explosion of camera flashes.

The models in front of her continued their fluid march

until only Nicole was left at the end.

She stopped. She posed. She waited.

Then she spun around and strutted after her girls. Still staring fiercely at nothing, her walk smooth and strong, her chin up.

Just like she was a supermodel's daughter.

Four

"It. Was. Brilliant!"

Gia's glowing outburst wasn't exactly unbiased– she'd have said it was brilliant no matter what– and though Nicole was certain her show hadn't been *bad*, she wasn't certain it had been any good.

She raised her eyebrows at Victoria and braced herself for the untarnished truth.

"I'd fund you," Victoria said, her highest compliment, and Nicole took a deep breath for the first time in days.

Gia clapped. "Now can we celebrate?"

"If you whip out a bag of candy. . ."

"Alcohol! Dancing!"

The room quieted abruptly and Nicole knew before turning around that her mother had entered.

"Nicole," the older woman said, then waited for her daughter to turn around before continuing. "Very daring. I loved it."

Everyone in the room started breathing again.

"Thank you, Nikita."

She'd always been Nikita. Not Mama or Mommy or Mom or Mother. She was Nikita, the one and only, to one and all.

And as if they were only recently introduced acquaintances, Nikita offered her cheek for an air kiss.

"I don't usually go out of my way to congratulate a debut designer," she said, smiling to those gathered around. "But I thought I could make an exception in this case."

Everyone laughed at her little joke.

"And your outfits were. . .interesting. Classic."

She took Nicole's hand and held it out to the side, studying the look she was still wearing, and Nicole said, "Thank you, Nikita."

Her mother smiled magnanimously, dropping Nicole's hand and then exiting the room.

Victoria said, "Now we can celebrate."

Nicole said, "With alcohol."

Five

Flynn spent the next morning checking equipment to be returned.

When that was done, he wandered around turning on computers and updating software, browsers. No one was going to come in today, he already knew. He doubted any of them were going to wake up today.

He ordered a new scanner and found someone's phone.

He changed a lightbulb. Not really his job but the buzzing drove him crazy enough to borrow a ladder from maintenance.

And then he went back to his closet to watch a few episodes of *The IT Crowd* with his feet up on his desk and his door *open*.

Yeah, this was the life.

He woke with a start, his chair shifting forward with his weight, and he flung his arms out in reflex. His stomach churned, his pulse raced, and then he was all the way awake and everything was okay.

He started laughing and then noticed Nicole Bissette

watching from the doorway.

Flynn jumped to his feet.

"Sorry! Fell asleep."

She looked at him and he smiled nervously. She always made him nervous with the looking.

He patted his still thumping heart. "I didn't think anyone was here."

"It's okay." She looked into the small room, his desk flush against one wall and his chair against the other.

It was a tight squeeze.

She said, "Do you have the video from yesterday?"

"Yeah, sorry. I didn't think you were coming in today. You know, celebrating?"

She nodded. And looked. And Flynn grabbed a thumb drive from his drawer and took one big step toward her to drop it in her hand.

"Thank you."

She turned and left and Flynn blew out his breath silently.

He froze with his mouth in open duck face when she came back into view.

"You can leave the door open. I'm the only one here today."

He closed his lips, then said, "Oh, okay. Thanks."

She nodded again, waiting and looking at him, and he finally realized what the problem was.

He shoved his hands into his pockets and said, "Flynn. My name."

She blinked, then her eyes softened. She looked like she was thinking about smiling.

And she said, "I know."

It was weird being here alone with her.

It was weird having his door open.

Normally, there was hustle and bustle. Designers and sewers and models, and today there was no one.

Nicole had also kept her door open and Flynn could hear the audio of her runway playing, over and over.

He felt like he should be doing something instead of watching reruns, so he refilled the paper in the printer.

And then he emptied the trash.

And then couldn't stand it anymore and went to knock on his boss's uncharacteristically open door. Her hair was in a loose bun and her rarely-seen glasses perched on her nose.

She looked like a librarian.

A librarian who should have been a model.

He shoved his hands in his pockets. "I've got nothing else to do today. You need anything? Want me to get your lunch?"

She took her glasses off, rubbing the bridge of her nose and shaking her head. "You can go home."

Maybe he'd go home and start looking for a new job. Something different. Something more.

He felt so tired even thinking about it because he seriously doubted there was anything more out there.

He turned and Nicole said, "Wait. Do you know anything about e-commerce?"

Flynn turned back around. "Like eBay and Etsy and WooCommerce?"

Nicole looked at him. "Like adding a store onto the website. How hard would that be?"

"Not hard at all. The hard part is getting people to know about it."

"Publicity. That's not the hard part."

Not for her, no.

She turned her chair around to look out the window.

"I wanted to get into stores, and I still do. That's what the last six months, what last night, was all about. But so many people have been talking about selling direct to consumers this show. They see it now, they want it now."

Flynn's heart sped up and he said, "You'd need an online store, product, payment processing, shipping capabilities."

She stared down at her desk, thinking, and he said, slowly, "I could do it."

Six

Flynn went home to Mom after that. For food and commiseration.

Where else did you go when you made a complete fool of yourself to your boss?

What else could you do when you didn't like beer and your buddies were all at work?

But his mom opened the door and was happy to see him and then proceeded to stuff him with leftovers until his dad got home.

When they heard the front door open, his mom called out, "Mike? Flynn came home for a visit."

His dad came around the corner. "You come on the train?" And when Flynn nodded, said, "You get fired?"

"Not yet. Probably tomorrow."

His dad sat down next to Flynn, sighing with relief at getting off his feet. "Good. You were being wasted there."

Lisa filled a plate for her husband. "Go wash. And leave him alone."

Mike patted his son's shoulder before getting back up. "You should look for something closer to home, out of the city. We could fix up the basement for you."

"Er. . ."

"He hasn't been fired yet, Mike."

"Just saying. It would be nice to have him close again." Mike washed his hands at the sink, wiping his hands dry on the kitchen towel. "When you have teenagers, you can't wait to get rid of them. And then they turn into men and don't want anything to do with you."

Lisa said pointedly, "Do you want to go live in *your* dad's basement?"

Mike grimaced and muttered, "We'd fix it up nice."

She laughed, pecking his cheek and finally sitting down to the table for the first time since Flynn had got there.

His dad tucked into his food, telling Flynn how his older brother had got a raise along with his new job as manager.

And his older sister, out in Idaho, was finally starting to enjoy the place after the culture shock of moving from Jersey to Boise.

All of it sounded like hell to Flynn, but it did seem like the natural progression of things.

And he knew why his dad wanted him to move into the basement.

The family was moving away, moving on. The family he'd sacrificed for, the family he'd worked his whole life for.

Sounded like hell.

Flynn had always sworn that he wouldn't waste his life. Wouldn't be chained to a desk, working with people he didn't like at a job that meant nothing.

And it had happened anyway. Because he didn't know what else there was.

Lisa said, "So tell us why you're going to get fired."

"I yelled at my boss."

"I hope it wasn't Nicole Bissette," she said and he

grimaced.

"Oh, Flynn. Why? She's so pretty but she always looks unhappy. You didn't need to yell at her."

Flynn raised his eyebrows at his mother and her cheeks warmed with color.

"Sometimes she's in *People*. I notice her just because you work for her."

Flynn remembered Nicole huddling beside the AV cart and said, "I don't think being a celebrity is all it's cracked up to be."

Mike took a big bite and said, "Especially not when their employees yell at them."

"And you were always such a sweet boy. I can't believe you yelled."

He couldn't believe it either. He'd wanted to do something besides change lightbulbs and she'd brought up the store and he'd gotten so excited.

All he did was manage her current website, about as challenging as turning phones off and on, and the thought of *creating* something made him want it. And then she'd said off-handedly, "Oh, we'll hire someone to do it."

He'd just snapped. Waving his arms around and sounding like a complete idiot.

"*What the hell did you hire me to do?* I sit in there like a lump, being wasted. I change toner and update software. *Use me.*"

Flynn closed his eyes, realizing he'd sounded just like his dad. Feeling useless and wasted and like his life was going nowhere and it didn't really matter because where would it go anyway.

Flynn said, "She's thinking about making an online store for the website and I told her I could do it."

His mom clapped her hands. "Oh, you'd be great at that. Remember the website you made in high school for the band. It was so clever."

He remembered.

"She didn't think I'd be great at it."

His dad said, "Then she's an idiot."

Flynn smiled at their show of support and when his mom pulled out a bag of cookies and filled a plate for him, his dad just shrugged his shoulders and said, resigned, "Those were my cookies."

"You don't need them. Flynn does."

When she turned her back, Flynn passed him a cookie under the table and Mike nodded his thanks.

"You going to stay the night?"

Flynn shook his head. "I'll have to catch the train tonight. I've got to show up at work in the morning to get fired."

Lisa hugged his shoulders from behind. "Oh, baby. It'll be just fine, you'll see."

"Mommm," Flynn whined, feeling about two years old.

She smoothed his hair and smiled. "You'll always be my baby."

His dad took pity on him, probably because of the cookie, and stood up. "Before you leave, can you take a look at my computer? It's taking a long time to start."

Flynn smiled.

"Yeah, Dad. I'll take a look."

Seven

Flynn was in his closet, hiding, the next morning when there was a knock on the door.

He stared at it, thinking he hadn't really been that bad yesterday.

Not worth firing.

He'd just maybe overstepped.

Knock knock.

He grimaced, then sighed, and was just about to get up and open the door when the knob turned. Nicole pushed open the door to look at him.

She looked behind her, then took a step inside. She shut the door and he said, "I'm sorry. I shouldn't have yelled at you."

She leaned against the wall and crossed one high-heeled boot over the other.

"And I wasn't really yelling *at* you, just. . .around you."

She said, "So, that was you yelling?"

"I'm sorry."

She cleared her throat. "You seemed very passionate, and I was thinking about what you yelled. I think you're right."

"It wasn't really yelling. . . You think I'm right?"

"I can't underutilize my employees."

He stood up and the closet suddenly seemed very small.

She didn't seem to notice. "Have you ever made a website before?"

"Yes."

"You should have led with that. Yesterday."

He said, stupidly truthful, "Not with a store before."

She nodded. "Do you think you can do it?"

"Yes."

"Okay. But this is just a trial. If I don't like it, I will outsource it."

"You'll like it."

He smiled and she didn't.

She's so pretty but she always looks unhappy.

She was and she did, and he said again, "Sorry about yesterday. I could have been passionate without the. . ."

He waved his arms, demonstrating, as if she could have possibly forgotten him doing it just yesterday. He nearly brushed her with his fingertips and he stopped abruptly.

She nodded. "I have time during lunch to discuss what I want."

"I'll be there."

Her lips twitched and she pushed herself away from the wall.

She pulled open the door, then turned back around.

"Do you need a bigger office?"

He shook his head because he'd suddenly realized how great his little closet was.

How visitors had to stand close to him, how he could smell the light perfume they wore that made him think of cookies.

How he was sure that scent would be lingering after they left.

He'd never had visitors actually come inside before. They just opened the door and talked to him and left.

And, you know, that was great, too.

Everything was great.

Today, everything was just great.

Eight

Nicole's assistant stuck her head in the door right before lunch and said, "Hey, your sister's here."

Since her sister was supposed to be in school, Nicole sighed. Then finished her email and nodded.

Her little sister flounced in wearing a lime-green shag sweater, a pink and purple striped miniskirt, and black garter stockings.

Nicole hoped she had a coat somewhere.

"What are you doing here?"

Colette flopped into a chair. "I came to yell at you."

"I mean, you should still be at school."

"We got out early."

Nicole didn't believe her. "Hmm."

"And I'm here to tell you that you need to fire your staff. I showed up to your show and they refused to let me in."

"I told them not to."

Colette sat up, outraged. "I was supposed to be one of the models!"

"You didn't show up for the fittings. Any of them. I found another girl."

"I'm your sister!"

"I'm *your* sister. And you couldn't bother to show up, to call, text, email, send a friend, come early the morning of the show. The resources at your seventeen-year-old fingertips are legion. You just didn't care that you were leaving me hanging."

"I didn't think I had to act like all the rest. I am your sister. And I'm the daughter of a supermodel. I don't need–"

"To be fitted?"

"I'm telling Nikita that you walk-blocked me on purpose," Colette said and Nicole let out a short bark of a laugh.

"Go ahead. What do you think she's going to say to a model who doesn't show up for a fitting?"

For an instant, Colette's bravado wavered. Say what you would about Nikita's mothering skills but as a model she'd been a professional. And she had choice words for models who weren't.

Colette's bravado came back quick enough though, and Nicole didn't know if that was age or personality.

Her sister said, "You'd love that, wouldn't you? You and Nikita could have something to talk about for more than thirty seconds."

Well, love was a strong word. It would certainly be interesting to have her mother's attention for that long.

"And I don't know why you went to all the trouble of your own show, anyway. Hire some designers and slap the Bissette name on it. That's what I'm going to do." Colette fluffed her hair, schooling her decade older sister. "You don't need to do it all yourself. Work smarter, not harder, Nicole. You're Nikita's daughter. Why work at all? Neither one of us has to."

She was right, and she was wrong. They had money,

trust funds. Maybe there wasn't a monetary need to work. But there was a psychological need to become something of one's own.

And Nicole was suddenly very, very tired because she knew Nicolette believed everything she'd just said.

Knew that she was happy to be the diminutive of her famous mother.

Nicole stood and began herding her sister out the door. "The daughter of Nikita is not really who I want to be my whole life. It's not enough for me; it's not enough for anyone. Now, if you don't mind, I have lots of work to do."

"You've got issues, you know that?"

"Yes. I like to pretend I have a few less than you."

Colette opened her eyes real wide, her pupils big and black, and said, "You don't."

"It's scary to think about, either way."

Nicole ordered lunch in and worked. She didn't understand her sister's lack of drive. When she'd been seventeen, Nicole had been working. Modeling, and finding out rather quickly that she was terrible at it.

She'd tried being a personal shopper– the go-to job of rich, bored, skill-less young women.

But again, terrible, and it was a blow to realize she was terrible at *shopping*.

Probably Nikita had despaired of her as she despaired of Colette.

Of course, Nicole hadn't been doing drugs when she was seventeen either. And she'd had a fierce need to be more than she was.

Prideful, that's what she was. Thinking there was something more than being a supermodel's daughter.

But she'd decided a long time ago that prideful was

better than useless.

She'd started assisting that year's hot fashion designer, her name opening doors that should have been closed to her– it's not what you know, it's who knows you– and she hadn't been terrible at it.

Had loved the sewing machines whirring. Had loved the colors and fabrics.

Had loved watching something wonderful being created from nothing but a vision.

Every step along the way looking rough and nothing like clothing.

And then when it was done, something beautiful.

She'd come home every night to pull apart another favorite piece of clothing. Dissect it and study it. Figure out why she'd bought it and why she'd wear it again and again when there were hundreds of other things to wear in her closet.

She loved clothes and fashion, and she'd take that from her mother without complaint.

Flynn knocked on her door, poking his head around the corner, and Nicole patted her lips and pushed her salad away.

She waved him in, trying hard not to stare at his ill-fitting and style-less clothing.

She'd never made it a requirement to be well-dressed to work here. Everyone *did.* They worked here because they loved clothing and fashion. They loved looking good and feeling good about it.

And then there was Flynn.

He sat down, pulling out a notebook. "So, what are you thinking for the store?"

"I hadn't got that far yet. It was a nebulous idea forming inside my mind before you insisted you be allowed to make it."

He put down his notebook and folded his arms.

They stared at each other and he said, "I thought you weren't upset about that."

She blew out a quiet breath. "Sorry. I'm cranky."

"Well, finish your lunch then. And I'll tell you what *I've* been thinking."

She was hungry, so she nodded and pulled her salad back over.

He said, "We'll match your website. Uncluttered, minimalist."

"I like that. The clothes are the focus."

"And we'll add a 'Shop at Nicole Bissette' banner on the homepage. The hard part is fulfillment, and we don't know what we'll need until we know what kind of volume we're talking about. Hundreds of items or a handful of items? One of a kind?"

"My mother is one-of-a-kind," she said, as if that answered his question, and she guessed it kind of did.

"Limited quantities, then."

She nodded. "Limited. High-end."

As if there had ever been any doubt about that.

She pulled up a rival designers website, clicking around.

"I don't like how they did that, too hard to find," she said and Flynn came around her desk to look over her shoulder.

"Three thousand dollars for a dress!"

Nicole hadn't noticed the price tag. "It's not outrageous."

"It is. It is actually the very definition of outrageous. I can go get a dictionary if you need proof."

And if Nicole laughed, she would laugh at that, at him.

"And why aren't the models smiling? Why do they have to look so miserable? If I was going to pay outrageous prices for a piece of clothing, I'd want to do it from happy, smiling models."

"They're not miserable, they're supposed to be invisible. Because it's about the clothes, not the models." She glanced behind her and looked pointedly at his slightly too short pants. "And you wouldn't buy nice clothing from any kind of model."

He wasn't offended at all at her snide remark, only nodded in agreement with her. "I've got much better things to spend my money on."

She was still looking at him, studying him, and he said, "It's no wonder you didn't become a model. You couldn't be invisible if you tried."

Oh, she had tried.

She turned back around. "It's because I have dead eyes. No model will last if she has dead eyes, even if she is Nikita's daughter."

"Dead eyes?" He came out from behind her desk and sat down again. "I've always thought they looked all-seeing. Like you could see everything everyone didn't want you to."

She blinked and sat back in her seat.

After a moment of silence, Flynn said, "Awk-ward. Back to the store."

Nicole pinched her lips together to keep from smiling.

"Back to the store. I'll have to decide what to price at. We'll need stock of all the sizes. A store may be more work than I was anticipating."

"We can do a test run. Put up one item, or just a couple of items, and work out the kinks."

She nodded slowly. "A soft launch."

"Ooh, do a Beyonce! Just put it up, see what happens."

"Don't announce it at all?"

He shook his head and Nicole said, "She's Beyonce. She

doesn't have to announce anything."

"And you're Nicole Bissette. You just had a successful NYFW show. Just release it. One item each and we'll put up a clock that shows how fast it gets sold out."

Nicole's eyes nearly popped out of her head. "Oh, I can just see that clock ticking on forever. Let's not do that."

Flynn laughed. "Come on."

"No."

"*Come on.*"

"No."

"And if no one buys it within twenty-four hours, we'll mark it as sold. If we can get it up now, while there's lots of interest from the show, they'll see it."

She squeezed her lips together, her stomach tightening in knots.

"It's impossible to get it up now. The clothes have to be made, the models have to be booked for photographs and I can tell you there aren't any left on the eastern seaboard this week. Oh, and *I'd need a store on my website*. Now is impossible."

"Say that all items ship in two to four weeks. I can get a temporary store put up in hours, there are templates available. And surely you know some models who can do you a favor on short notice."

She shook her head, then stopped.

". . .maybe my sister."

"Or you could do it. You did the runway."

"And that was a mistake, obviously."

"Well, if invisible is what you were going for, then yes. And what about Nikita? Make it a family affair?"

Nicole couldn't stop the laugh that escaped.

Flynn grinned at her. "I'd pay $3000 to see Nikita modeling your stuff."

She laughed again, then shook her head.

"I'm not even going to ask her. But I might have a couple of friends who could model for me on short notice. You really think we could have something up this week?"

"It'll be a simple design but I can have it up in hours."

"They'll need to be able to choose sizes and inseams for each piece. Can you do that?"

"*I find your lack of faith disturbing.*" He grinned. "I'm kidding. I can do that."

"Is it going to look dumb?"

"No. Simple."

She breathed out a long breath. Thought about really going after this. And said, "Not the clock. I just know that will be terrible for my mental health."

Nine

Flynn got to work. A rush of energy and excitement hit him so hard that he floated back to his closet.

He read reviews, poured through code, and surfed forums because someone had already done everything on the internet and it was always for sale.

Hours later, he ran back to Nicole's office before she left for the night.

"I need your credit card. Or PayPal. Or a picture of you naked. Any or all of those are considered valid currency on the internet."

She just stared at him until he flushed and muttered, "I was just kidding about that last one."

He hadn't been.

And the way she was looking at him made him think she knew it, too.

But she followed him wordlessly and paid for it.

Flynn cracked his knuckles and said with glee, "Okay, now to make it ours."

She watched him for a few minutes and when she left, he waved absentmindedly.

He hoped she hadn't been talking to him.

And when she came back in the next morning, he was still working.

She stared at his untucked shirt and wild hair. "Did you work all night?"

He grinned like a maniac. "Red Bull and coffee. I can't feel my feet."

She tugged at his chair. "Please go home and get some sleep."

"Not done. Still prettying it up. You want to see it?"

"It's not live, is it?"

He shook his head, turning his laptop so she could see. He opened a browser window and there was her store.

Nice, simple. It matched the feel of her website. It looked professional.

It had smiling models wearing bathing suits.

"I just cut and pasted so I could see what it'd look like. We'll need sales copy to go along with your pictures."

Nicole rubbed her forehead. "I'll add it to the list."

"It's good, huh?"

Nicole looked at it again, leaning toward the screen and him.

"It's good. Sizes, inseams, colors. Better than I thought it would be."

"I'm still working on the banner."

She put her hand on his shoulder. "Go home, it doesn't need to be done right this second. I still have to find some models."

He nodded and she left, and Flynn fell asleep on his desk.

"Oh, my back."

Flynn sat himself up, creaking and moaning. His eyes were scratchy and there was cotton in his mouth and he quoted to his empty closet, "*I'm too old for this shit.*"

He pulled himself to his feet and staggered through the door, the light suddenly blinding him. When he could see again, the office was unexpectedly full of activity– sewing machines whirring and fabric being cut. Nicole in the middle of it all, looking through photos of outfits and models.

Everyone stopped to stare at him.

Nicole handed off the photos and came to him, her normal *is that what you're wearing* expression looking more like *who let this yeti in?*

She didn't stop when she got to him, just grabbed his arm and walked him toward her office.

"I thought you went home."

"Fell asleep." He nodded at the hubbub behind them. "How long was I out for?"

"It's still today, if that's what you're asking."

He grinned. "Oh, good. You've been busy."

"I was inspired by how much you accomplished in one night. We're picking the five outfits we think will sell the best and are making three sizes of each. That should be enough of a start, right?"

He nodded. "We'll just mark the rest sold out."

"Good. I've begged my friends to come model for me. And promised my soul to a photographer to get him to show up tomorrow on such short notice."

She shut her office door behind them and turned to him. She crossed her arms. Then sighed.

"At least you didn't sleep in your suit jacket. Take your shirt off."

"Huh?"

She stepped all up into his personal space, her perfume wafting into his nose and short-circuiting his brain.

She undid his tie, pulling it from his neck and laying it

gently on the back of a chair.

He was still standing there stupidly when she reached out to unbutton his shirt.

"Whoa, what. . . I'm still sleeping, aren't I?"

She rolled her eyes. "No. You're a mess."

She slid his shirt down his arms, shaking it and taking it to the row of storage cabinets behind her desk. She opened a door, taking out a hangar, an iron, a bottle of Febreze.

She grabbed a packet of baby wipes and handed it to him.

He looked down at it and she said, "Pants, please."

"No, thanks."

"They need to be ironed. . .well, they need to be thrown away but ironing is all I can do at the moment."

"They're fine."

She said, with steel in her voice, "I'm stronger than I look."

Flynn took a small step back. "Well, jeez. Turn around or something."

She did, hanging up his shirt and spritzing it.

She pulled down a mini ironing board, turned on the iron.

She turned around again just as he was pulling a leg of his pants off. "Hey!"

She choked back her laughter and grabbed for his tie.

"Flynn, I've been around models, male and female, since before I could walk. I've seen it."

"Not mine, you haven't," he said, as if he could possibly be proud of *not* ever being naked in front of her.

But she was turned around again, spritzing his tie and shaking his shirt, and he didn't have to think about it for too long.

She turned around again as he was pulling off the other leg.

He glared at her. "Okay, now I know you're doing it on purpose."

She laughed that time, no choking it back, and she scooted around him to grab a stack of fashion magazines.

"I just had to make sure I wasn't imagining that your boxers were plaid."

He looked down, grabbing the gaping front and mustering all the courage he had, to say with as much dignity as he could, "What the hell color are they supposed to be?! No one's supposed to see them anyway!"

She smiled at his flustered exclamation as she scooted past him again, grabbing his pants from his hand and saying, "Wipe."

He started wiping his chest and underarms muttering about women, especially women in *fashion*, who lose all sense of decency and decorum. Prancing around half naked all the time and expecting everyone else to do the same.

Her shoulders were shaking as she did his pants and then checked his shirt and tie again.

"Be right back," she said. "I'm going to get your jacket."

And he yelled as she opened the door, "*Come on*! Am I getting punked?"

Flynn was trying to hide behind her chair, still wearing just his plaid underwear, when she came back in smiling.

She ironed his jacket quickly, saying, "It's not in too bad of shape."

"That's because I don't wear it."

She looked over her shoulder at him, his underwear safe from her prying eyes. "Are you okay now?"

"No, I'm traumatized."

"I didn't see anything."

"Yeah, right."

"If I give you my robe to wear, can I do your hair?"

He looked down. "Pretty sure anything of yours is not

going to fit me."

"Sit down and I'll drape it over you."

He waited for her to turn around again before sitting down and crossing his legs and arms in front of him protectively.

She took out a long pale peach robe, draping it over him from shoulders to knees and he sighed in relief.

He said, "You have to freshen yourself up a lot in here?"

"Yes. And *I* don't prance around half naked in my office."

She smiled at him, a close mouthed grin that showed off a dimple he hadn't known she had. And before he could come up with a smart answer to that, she'd grabbed two wipes and was vigorously rubbing his head between her hands.

"I-I-I d-d-don't ha-a-ate this-s-s."

When his hair was damp, she grabbed a small bottle sprayer filled with–

"Wait, what's in it?"

"Water."

"You may proceed."

–water and spritzed lightly, running her fingers through his hair.

Flynn closed his eyes in near ecstasy, and missed when she squirted a dollop of gel onto her palms.

He smelled it, though, when she started rubbing it into his hair.

"Aw, come on. I hate gel."

"Why?"

"Because I look like a guy with gel in my hair when I wear it."

"Trust me."

"I would have, if you hadn't kept sneaking glances of

my boxers."

She smushed his hair this way and that, again and again, not denying that she had sneaked her peeks.

He waved at his head. "You do this every day?"

"Sometimes multiple times."

"And you like it?"

"I think it's important to look good. I think it's fun to make myself pretty."

Fun was not a word he connected with Nicole, so he smiled at her and said, "Good. You don't always look like you're having fun."

Her eyes met his. "The same could be said for you."

"True." He sighed, then said, "I had fun last night."

"Good. Even if it did make you look like a wild man staggering out of a forest."

"Wild and hairy?"

"Yes. I had no choice but to try and make you presentable." She grabbed a comb. "I do like coming in to work every day even if I don't look like it. I like making pretty things."

He remembered her curled up beside the AV cart and said, "You didn't like doing the runway."

She picked at his hair until it looked how she wanted it to look, then grabbed a wipe and started cleaning up her hands. "I don't like being looked at."

He eyed her, so beautiful she could stop a man's heart cold.

"Must be tough to be you, then."

She just looked at him, and he realized she hadn't done that looking thing in a while.

"I thought I had to do the runway because it was *next*. I've never really had a plan, just done whatever was offered to me. I've never known where I wanted to go, just knew it was somewhere."

And that sounded so much like himself that he just said, "Yeah."

"And sometimes I don't know that I don't want to do something until I'm in the middle of doing it."

He nodded slowly. "Oh, I get that. For example, I didn't realize I wouldn't enjoy taking my pants off in your office until I was halfway done."

The smile came back into her eyes, if not back onto her face, and she said, "I apologize for peeking."

"I accept your apology. But it's only fair if I get a peek of yours."

She looked, again, then smiled.

"Okay."

She bent down close to him, putting her hand on his jaw and rubbing gently. She said softly, "Baby wipe. It's stuck in your stubble."

She blew lightly on his face, and Flynn was too busy trying to see her bra to say anything in reply.

She said, "It looks good on you."

He looked up. "Baby wipe?"

"Stubble. Some men's comes in splotchy, but yours looks good."

Flynn grunted and whispered, "This peek is no good. I can't see your bra."

"I know. I designed this blouse and it irritates me to have it gape open every time I need to get into my purse. It irritates me even more to see my bra in tomorrow's tabloid."

"So this wasn't you giving me a peek?"

"No. A peek is clandestine. Showing you isn't a peek."

He opened his mouth and said, "Aaargh."

She patted his cheek and stood back up. "I'll owe you one."

She went back to his clothes, ironing them meticulously

and then handing them over.

Flynn dressed quickly, happy to be clothed like he'd never been before, and he didn't even complain when Nicole turned around before he'd finished buttoning his shirt.

She stopped him, sliding her hands inside and dabbing the cologne sample she'd neatly ripped from one of her magazines against his skin.

"It's not quite *you* but beggars can't be choosers."

"I'm wearing gel and cologne. It's definitely not me."

She buttoned his shirt for him and tied his tie and helped him into his jacket, and he had to admit, to himself at least, that he didn't hate that either.

Nicole folded a swatch of fabric into a neat square and tucked it into his breast pocket, then pulled him toward the full-length mirror hanging inside one door.

She stood him in front of it, turning him this way and that and critiquing him silently. Finally, she shrugged.

"Well. You'll have to wear it ironically."

"You know I'm going home in like an hour. What was the point of doing all this for just an hour?"

"You'll see. Look better, feel better. Look great, feel great. Can I design a suit for you? I've never made menswear before."

"That's because men won't pay three thousand for a pair of pants."

She patted his side. "You'd be surprised."

He probably would be because he thought his cheap suit looked pretty good.

And he grudgingly admitted, "The hair's not bad."

"Sometimes I know what I'm doing."

But. "I hate the cologne."

She agreed. "It's not right."

She grabbed his hand and tugged him to and out the

door. She didn't stop until she was in front of her staff and presenting him like she was Vanna White unveiling her newest vowel.

And when everyone looked and gasped and clapped, Flynn said, "Great. Thank you. Now, I need to see a man about a Red Bull."

Ten

Nicole watched Flynn walk around like he'd suddenly realized he was the lone man in the office. His back was straight and when the printer wouldn't print, he puffed out his chest and took care of it.

Look better, feel better.

Maybe it was superficial and shallow but she knew the power of put together.

Look great, feel great.

She'd have to really start thinking about menswear. Flynn wore suits because that's what he was supposed to do not because he loved them, and she wondered if she could make him a suit he would love. She felt the challenge of it calling to her, and she quickly reined it in to focus on the challenge she'd already started.

Tomorrow she had the photographer coming, and Victoria and Gia had agreed to model for her.

Gia had squealed with excitement and asked what else she could do to help. Victoria had bartered for one of Nicole's runway designs for her services, and Nicole was lucky they didn't wear the same size shoe or she would have lost her favorite boots as well.

Flynn stopped in her doorway before he left for the night and Nicole smiled at him. "You should go clubbing. You look too good to just go home."

"See, that's the problem with gel in the hair. People start thinking you *club*." He nodded at the phone in her hand. "Are you going home soon?"

"Yes, I'm just trying to call my sister. She wanted to model for me, so I'm giving her a second chance. If she'll ever answer her phone."

"I'll stick around for the show if you're going to call Nikita and ask her to model for you."

"Bye-bye." She waved at him and he grinned, turning away. When he was out of sight, she yelled after him, "I know you like the gel in your hair!"

"I hate it! I'm going home to wash it out right now!"

Nicole chuckled, then hung up with a put-upon sigh when her sister's phone went to voicemail again.

She wasn't going to call Nikita, because a show it would be. But she wouldn't be home from work and maybe Colette would be. At home. After school. . .

Probably not, but their loft was on Nicole's way home anyway. It wouldn't hurt to at least stop and see. Offer an olive branch.

And give her sister something to *do*.

Colette *was* home, and when she opened the door Nicole just blinked at her and said, "Oh. Hey."

"Hey."

"I didn't think you'd be home."

"I'm going out. Soon."

Colette turned away, leaving the door open for her sister to close softly behind her.

"I called you."

"Yeah?"

"I'm doing a shoot tomorrow and I need models. I *am* sorry you couldn't do the show, and I thought this might make up for it."

Nicole followed Colette through the loft to her bedroom, standing awkwardly as her sister sat down at her vanity.

Colette said, "Eh. I'm over it."

Nicole took a deep breath. "You're over it? You were in my office yesterday yelling at me."

"It sucked. I was left standing outside my very own sister's show like a lameass. But I've got things tomorrow so. . . Thanks for the offer?"

Thanks for the offer?

You're welcome, you ungrateful little. . .

Nicole watched her sister put her makeup on, almost meditatively, and it reminded her of watching her mother.

And feeling the exact same *why do I even bother*.

Nicole turned away, catching a glimpse of white hanging on the closet door.

"Please tell me you are not wearing that, wherever it is you're going tonight."

Colette looked into the mirror at the white bustier and finally showed some emotion.

She turned around, excited. "Want to see it on?"

Nicole shook her head no but Colette was already pushing past her. "Be right out!"

And a few minutes later, she was standing in the doorway wearing all white– bustier, skintight hot pants, open-toed boots that laced up to her knees, and fingerless gloves.

"Has Nikita seen you in this?" Nicole asked, and at her sister's nod sighed hopelessly.

"Our mother is a failure as a parent."

"What are you talking about? I look amazing!"

"You look like you should be dancing in a red window."

Colette looked down happily. "I was going for virgin whore."

And all Nicole could say was, "Yes."

"I'm going to a party at the marina. The Wind Weaver yacht. And I probably won't be recovered by tomorrow, so that's why I can't help you with your shoot."

Sounded horrible to Nicole but her sister was talking, at least.

"Who's all going?"

"*Everyone*. Jonas got his dad to pay for Afrojack to come DJ, can you believe it?"

"Wait. Are you going *with* Jonas. He's only a few years younger than me."

"He's twenty-five. Older guys are hot."

"You're *seventeen*."

"Age is just a number. And I'll be eighteen in three months."

"So wait until then to date a twenty-five-year-old!"

Colette snorted. "Please. It's not like he's my first."

And she sounded so old, so cynical that the air just rushed from Nicole. She whispered, "Colette."

"What? I'm going on his *yacht*. I'd date him if he was thirty-five."

"His father's yacht," Nicole corrected, her stomach churning, and Colette rolled her eyes.

"Okay, his father's yacht. Same thing."

"It's not. It's really, really not."

"OMG. I do not want to hear this again. I know what you think of me, okay Nicole? I'm lazy and I'm vain."

"I don't think that."

"But I've got plans. My own plans. I'm not going to be Nikita. And I'm not going to be Nicole. *Careful Nicole.*"

She whirled around and into her bathroom, slamming the door behind her.

Nicole jumped, then blew out a long breath. She watched the door for a long minute and when she decided her sister wasn't ever coming back out again, looked around the room.

It used to be hers. A *very* long time ago.

She pushed open the closet door, slowly. Telling herself that she was only looking. Only wanted to see if there was anything in her sister's closet that wasn't short or tight.

She fingered a long skirt, pulling it out to hold it up to the light, and murmured, "Or see-through."

She put it back, and looked at the clothes hanging where her bed had been.

This closet had been her home.

It was big enough that she could have fit a real bed in here, but everyone liked to pretend she didn't sleep in the closet. All curled up on a nest of blankets.

Safe, with two locked doors between her and everyone else.

She closed the door from inside, crouching to examine the screw holes that had never been patched over. And she laughed softly, thinking that little lock she'd painstakingly screwed into the door and frame couldn't have kept out anyone who really wanted in.

But it had made her *feel* safe.

Until her sister got old enough to undo it. Old enough to not be placated with dolls and board games. Old enough to not want to be hiding in the closet when there was music blaring and bodies thumping and voices screaming with laughter.

Old enough to have to make Nicole choose over and over again between hiding in her closet or going after her little sister. Out there.

Nicole sighed, pushing herself back up and opening the door.

Colette shrieked and a zipped baggie went flying out of her hand.

Nicole looked down at the baggie and Colette fell against the wall, holding her hands to her chest.

"You scared me! I thought you'd left."

"Colett–"

"I told you I had plans!" Colette recovered enough to bend down and scoop the baggie up. "Live hard; die young. Twenty-seven, baby."

"Don't even joke about that."

"Who's joking? Jim Morrison, Kurt Cobain, Amy Winehouse. Forever young, and they all died at twenty-seven."

Nicole knew. Everyone knew about the 27 Club.

When Nicole didn't say anything, Colette laughed. High and shrill.

"OMG. You totally think I'm *serious*!"

Nicole just stood there, not saying anything. Unable to say anything.

Her baby sister high and wild and oblivious.

Nicole couldn't be around her, couldn't stand to be reminded how it used to be with her mother.

High and wild and oblivious.

Frightening.

Nicole had protected her sister as well as she could. And then Nicole had left to go to boarding school and it had been a relief.

To get away from them both.

She turned to leave, get away again.

Colette said to her back. "I don't know how you can stand to be yourself. So uptight. You'll live forever, miserable, because you just can't let go!"

Nicole slapped back with her words as she left, just like she'd left when she was fourteen because she didn't know what else she could do.

"And when you OD at twenty-seven, you still won't be part of that club, Colette. You have to be somebody to be in that club, not just the daughter of somebody."

Eleven

Flynn did not put gel in his hair the next morning.

If under oath, he might have admitted to thinking about what he was putting on as he got dressed for work but he'd swear on a bible that was as far as it went.

He did make sure his underwear was presentable but that was just self-preservation. A guy had to be prepared to end up in Nicole Bissette's office half naked, apparently.

And no bible would make him say that he'd glanced at a few well-dressed suits on the subway.

Suits. No, thanks. He didn't ever want to be one.

He *wore* one because he had to. And yeah, he liked to think he wore it ironically like Nicole had said.

But he wouldn't ever *be* a suit.

He wondered if there was a job out there where he didn't even have to wear one but it fell right out of mind when he got to work to find it teeming with people.

Photographer and assistant setting up. Seamstresses putting finishing touches on clothing. A makeup artist trying to put lipstick on one of the models who was flapping her arms and arguing loudly with another model who was getting her long brown hair styled.

Nicole stood between them, the calm eye of the storm, and when she noticed him, her eyes traveled down to his shoes– okay, he might have dusted them off– and back up again to his hair.

She raised an eyebrow at him and he mouthed to her, "No gel. I'll quit."

Her lips twitched and then she shrugged one shoulder gallantly. He meandered close enough to hear her say, "You're safe. Today."

He nodded at the arguing models. "Anything I can fix?"

"Not unless you have a time machine that could go back ten minutes or so."

Flynn patted his pockets. "Mmm, I left it in my other pants. Sorry."

The model who was getting her hair done turned around to look at him.

Her eyes traveled down and then her eyes traveled back up, and what Flynn had found fun and slightly endearing from Nicole was aggressive and cold from her.

She said, "*This* is Flynn?"

The wild-haired model with the waving limbs stopped yelling and turned around, too.

She looked at him, her eyes zigzagging from left top to right bottom, and she said, "That's too bad about the time machine. You could have stopped a perfectly good friendship from being flushed down the toilet."

Nicole held out one hand. "Victoria." And the other. "And Gia. My best friends, who agreed to model for me on super short notice."

Victoria turned back around, choosing to study Flynn in the mirror. It wasn't anymore pleasant an experience for him.

Gia turned her chair completely around and the makeup artist stifled a sigh, following her with her lipstick brush.

"Ex-best friend."

Victoria stopped sizing up Flynn long enough to flick her eyes at Gia.

"Why are you taking it out on Nicole? I was the one who said it."

Gia sniffed, ignoring Victoria, and Nicole was the one who answered.

"Because I was supposed to tell you that you were wrong. And you're not."

Gia sucked in a breath. "Oh, I hate you so much right now. And I am a size effing 12, not plus-sized!"

Flynn took a step back, realizing fairly quickly that this was a conversation he wanted no part of.

Nicole glanced at him and said calmly, "You're scaring him."

"Plus-sized!"

Victoria said, "I called you a plus-sized *model*. Anything above a 6 is considered plus-sized."

Gia threw her hands in the air. "That. Is. Effed. Up!"

Flynn said, "I'm going to go see if I put my spare time machine in my closet."

Nicole patted his arm, making Victoria's eyes narrow and Gia sit back in her chair.

"I'll call you if we need–" Nicole began and then the photographer's assistant ran over, telling them they were ready for the first model.

Victoria rose, suddenly all business and forgetting about Flynn. Nicole walked around her, checking to make sure she was perfect, and then they walked over together, Victoria saying it had been awhile since she'd done modeling but she was sure it would come back to her.

Gia was quiet long enough for the makeup artist to finish and Flynn stood watching, trying to see in his mind's eye how the final pictures would look on the website.

Gia interrupted his thinking.

"I've been friends with them for over a decade and you know what conclusion I've come to?" Flynn turned to her and she said, "Money effs you up. Lots of money effs you up lots."

"Okay."

"It makes you untrusting, closed. Mean, sometimes. Afraid, other times. You think everybody wants what you have, and you're not wrong."

Flynn had no idea where this conversation was going so he said okay again.

"You like her," she said, more a universal observation than a question, and Flynn suddenly understood.

"Ohhhhh." And Flynn couldn't even really argue with her. He liked Nicole. But he was a man, so he considered the situation the same as breathing.

He was a man, he was alive, of course he liked her.

Gia raised an eyebrow at him. "She's Nicole Bissette. She's been hit on more times than you've woken up. Are you thinking about joining that long list?"

"Err. . ."

He hadn't been thinking about it for real. Fantasizing about it, maybe, but she was Nicole Bissette.

"I think you should. You seem nice."

He blinked, trying not to be embarrassed. And suddenly, once again, not knowing where this conversation was going.

"And if you're not nice, Victoria will rip the skin from your bones so I don't really have to worry about whether you really *are* nice or if you just seem that way."

Flynn blinked again, looking over his shoulder at Victoria.

"Nicole's been hit on a jillion gazillion times but never

said yes. And she hasn't had a boyfriend in. . .ever. . .so there you go. I give you my blessing. Hop on in there."

"I have no idea what to say to that. Except maybe that I'd like to go to my closet."

Gia ran her eyes up and down his poor suit again. "You ever seen the movie *Hitch*?"

"Yeah."

"You should watch it again. Take some notes because you're a regular guy. And I know what it's like to be around royalty when you're not. They're just. . .from a different country. You've got to learn how to speak their language, Flynn. And I'd help you but I'm leaving Monday, so watch *Hitch*."

He didn't say anything more, didn't want to give her anymore encouragement.

Didn't want her to give him anymore encouragement.

Because he couldn't ask out Nicole Bissette. She was his boss!

Flynn had carefully shuffled a couple feet away by the time Nicole and Victoria finished. They headed back to makeup and Gia jumped up from her chair.

Nicole inspected her outfit and as they walked away, Gia said again, "Plus-sized."

"I didn't call you that. I called you my best friend doing me a favor."

"And how come you're not up here modeling your own clothes?"

Before Flynn could hear her answer, he turned, hoping to make his escape, and found Victoria standing right behind him, her hands on her hips. She said, "Outfit change. Wanna watch?"

Flynn jerked back and Victoria smiled at him.

"Whatever Gia told you I'd do to you, believe it."

Flynn pointed over her shoulder toward his closet. "I'm

just gonna. . ."

"And after that, I'll really get started."

"I'm not–"

"Interested in her?"

"Well–"

"Going to try anything?"

"Of course–"

"Hurt her?"

"No."

Victoria continued to stare into his eyes, then she looked behind him.

"She likes you. She talks about you."

Flynn whirled around to stare at Nicole before he'd even thought about it. Nicole met his eyes, raising her eyebrows at him.

When he just shook his head, she frowned at Victoria, then turned back to Gia, telling her to stop smiling.

Gia shook out her hair. "Plus-sized model, Nic. That means fat and *happy*."

Flynn said softly, mostly to himself because he wasn't sure he wanted Victoria to answer, "Did she say she liked me?"

Victoria breathed into his ear. "No. I'm saying it."

"Why?"

"I can already tell that between the two of you, there's no one to make the first move. So here's a little push."

Flynn looked again at Nicole's face, not seeing any kind of liking on it then turned back around to face her friend. And take a big step back.

He said, "You just want me to make a fool of myself."

Victoria smiled. "That does seem like something I'd do," she said, and Flynn didn't know why crazily beautiful women had to be all crazy.

She said, "But it's hard to tell what Nicole likes because

of her Resting Bitch Face."

Flynn's fists balled. "Hey!"

Victoria seemed amused. "What? We helped her perfect it. *Stop. No. Not welcome.*"

Nicole said right behind Flynn, "It doesn't always work."

He looked behind him at her face that was right now saying to Victoria: *Stop. No. Not welcome.*

He said, "It doesn't?"

Nicole said to Victoria, "Go over there and get Gia to stop smiling so much."

"Oh, it'll be my pleasure."

Flynn watched Victoria strut away and Nicole said softly, "Sorry. They're overwhelming sometimes, I know."

Flynn nodded. Overwhelming was one word for it.

He said, "I'm going to go hide in my closet until everyone is gone. If you need–"

Gia shouted at Victoria, "You need to apologize because if I leave while we're fighting, we'll never get over it!"

Nicole whirled around. "Leaving?"

Gia chewed on her upper lip. "I'm going to Florida."

"No!"

"I need to. It's my nonna. She's getting older, you know, and I always said I would go back home after school and I never did and then she moved to Florida with my uncle. I *promised*."

"Are you going to come back?"

Gia shrugged, sad. "I don't know. I didn't really find what I was looking for here. Maybe I'll find it in Florida."

The photographer raised his hands as if to say, *hey, I'm working here*, and Flynn shook his head at him. *Do not get in the middle of this. Trust me.*

"I've told you that you can come work for me," Victoria said and Gia looked over at Flynn, wide-eyed.

"You've known us for a few minutes now. Can you think of anything worse for the universe than me working for Victoria?"

Flynn tried not to laugh, and absolutely refused to answer.

Nicole said, "You can come work for me then."

Gia said softly, "I'm not looking for a job. . .or *only* a job. I'm looking for someplace I belong. New York isn't it. But thanks for giving me something to laugh about when I miss you guys."

Nicole sat down heavily. "You should have told us you were even thinking of leaving."

"I know but I just kept hoping it wouldn't come together. Nothing ever has before, why would this be any different?"

Victoria looked carefully at Nicole.

"This is probably a bad time to tell you that I'm going out to San Francisco for a while."

Nicole gripped the arms of the chair and Gia said, "Angel of death?"

Victoria corrected her. "Angel of mercy."

"Same thing."

"Sometimes."

Nicole said softly, "What about your father?"

"He's coming with me. I've got an in-home nurse lined up."

"You're going to be gone a long time then."

"This one needs me there, hands-on. The business is being run by a bunch of morons but they've got some great medical patents. If I can't save the business, I'll strip those out and sell 'em to someone who knows what to do with them."

Gia closed her eyes, shaking her head. "Why does anyone come to you as their angel investor?"

"Because I'm the best. And I can save them. And they're desperate. Desperate people make bad deals."

"So you take advantage of their desperation?"

"No. I make a good deal. If they were less stupid, they would make a better deal."

"See?" Gia said to Flynn. "Effed up. It gets passed on in the blood."

Victoria said, "Mm, says the woman going home to live with her family I assume?"

"Just for a little while. I've got a temporary job lined up. Fashion consultant."

Nicole pushed herself from the chair, making her way back to her friends. "That's code for personal shopper."

"I can charge more if I use fashion consultant. I can charge even more because I'm a *New York* fashion consultant."

Victoria smiled. "I always knew there was a reason I liked you. I'm glad we finally figured it out." Gia returned the smile until Victoria added, "Did your cousin set it up for you?"

"Shut up. It was my sister-in-law."

"Work those connections, Gia. I'm glad you've got someone to look out for you down there because the only way you made it through an all-girls school *and* New York City is you had us watching out for you."

"I know. Why didn't you let them eat me?"

"The world needs gummy bears."

Gia put her arms around her friend, squeezing. "Aw. See? There is a heart in there."

"Eh. Florida is going to ruin your hair."

Nicole sniffed, joining in the hugfest. "It's going to be *terrible*."

And Gia wailed, "I know!"

The photographer looked through his lens at the three

women hugging each other and said, "I can probably make this work."

Twelve

Flynn watched *Hitch*.

In his closet, while putting the finishing touches on the store, all the while wondering if this movie was supposed to help him at all.

Because all he got from it was to be yourself but pretend to be someone else. And be sure to be confident about it.

Yeeaahhh.

Not that he wanted to date Nicole. . .

No, really. He didn't.

He liked her. Maybe.

She was gorgeous. Absolutely.

But she was Nicole Bissette and he didn't know how anyone could live their life front and center like she had to.

And she had beautiful crazy friends, let's not forget that important fact.

But he was like a moth to a flame. He kept coming back to the idea and he couldn't stay away from her and he wouldn't be able to until she zapped him.

When he was as finished with the store as he could be without her final input, he knocked on her door lightly.

Enjoying the anticipation of seeing her again and making it last as long as possible, and when she called out, he opened the door slowly.

She looked up from her desk and Flynn remembered what her friend had called that look of hers. *Resting Bitch Face.*

And okay, he could see it. And the point of it.

He just didn't happen to see it right this minute, and his heart sped up.

"I'm done with the store. Just need you to okay it."

"Why don't you come show me. I need a break right now anyway."

He came around her desk, leaning over to type in the URL and password.

Her scent floated up, into his head, and he thought, *Don't sniff her, dumbass.*

He said gruffly, "Just let me know the things you're not a hundred percent happy with."

She took a moment to click links and try adding items to the cart.

"It's beautiful. You've mimicked the website perfectly." She looked over her shoulder at his clothes. "I think you have real style, I don't know why you dress like that."

"You're not going to put gel in my hair again, are you?"

She sniffed, turning back around and pointing at the screen. "Let's change this to prêt-à-porter."

"Ready to wear?" She looked at him in surprise and he said, "It's a movie. Can't you just say ready to wear?"

"No. I'm French," she said, then mimicked her friend from yesterday. "And I can charge more if it's in French."

"How are you French?"

"My mother was born in France? Ergo, French?"

"Ergo?" He shook his head in defeat. "I'll give you French-American."

She chuckled, still trying not to smile and saying, "French-American? What does that make you, Geek-American?"

He laughed, shaking his head. "I prefer Geekus Tyrannicus."

"Geekus Tyrannicus?" She finally broke, her laugh escaping in little huffs, her smile lighting her entire face, her full lips opening slightly, and brown eyes warming.

Flynn's breath caught and he just stared.

Nicole looked at the expression on his face and the smile disappeared. "Sorry."

Flynn nodded mindlessly and tried restarting his brain. "Yeah."

Nicole turned away. "Now you know why I don't smile."

He shook his head to clear it. "I can see how having all the men within your vicinity brainless would get old. I mean, you're gorgeous all the time. But when you smile. . ."

"I know, I look like Nikita."

And maybe that was it. Maybe having a living, breathing woman look at you just like the poster you'd had taped above your bed while growing up was what it was. Fantasy turned real.

Right here in front of him. Close enough to smell.

Stop sniffing her, you idiot!

Nicole reached across her desk and grabbed a box of Kleenex to hand back to him.

He flushed. "Sorry. I think it's your perfume."

"It's vanilla body wash."

"Smells good."

She shook her head. "Just plain vanilla."

He couldn't help himself. He leaned down and took a long, long sniff.

He said softly, "Smells good."

"That's all I am, Flynn. Vanilla. Even if I look like a *Nikita*." At his blank look, she added, "Nikita has a perfume."

"Ah. You should make one, too. You'd make a fortune."

The corner of her mouth twitched. "I'd make a fortune with plain vanilla?"

He'd give her all his money right now if she let him sniff her again. So he said, "Yes."

She chuckled. "Well, thank you for the store. Maybe it'll make me that fortune."

He nodded. "It's what I'm here for. To do everything, and nothing."

She cocked her head. "You don't do nothing. You do everything. Anytime we need anything, we call on you."

"I thought that was because I did nothing and was available."

She put her hand on his forearm. "You really think you do nothing here?"

"I have no idea why you hired me."

She gave him a slight smile. "It's funny how we think we know what others think of us. *I* don't know how this place would stay running without you."

Flynn digested that. Then said, "You should give me a raise."

"Let's not get carried away."

He raised a crooked eyebrow. "Can you guess what I'm thinking about you right now?"

She laughed at him, and maybe Flynn was getting used to his brain short-circuiting because he hardly stopped breathing at all.

She said, "I don't have to guess what people think of me. I only have to read the tabloids to find out."

"You don't have to guess about me either since I

already told you. I think you could sell plain old vanilla like it was diamonds, and any minute now I'm going to stop caring you're not going to give me a raise just because you smell so good."

She leaned toward him, waving her arm in front of him so he could smell her vanilla body wash, and whispered, "Any minute now?"

Flynn knew that right about here is where Nicole needed to whip out her Resting Bitch Face.

Stop. No. Not welcome.

Right before he did something stupid.

He stared down at her, and she looked up at him. And he was pretty sure she knew what he was thinking about her.

Pretty sure she was getting it right.

And then, she looked away. She cleared her throat. And slowly, sat back in her chair.

I can already tell that between the two of you, there's no one to make the first move.

Sad thing was, Crazy Beautiful was right.

No one here was going to make the first move.

Flynn decided he'd be philosophical about it. He'd decide it was better this way.

He could look, and sniff, and dream.

And it was *better*.

Because getting zapped probably wasn't as much fun as it sounded.

Thirteen

Flynn made the final touches on the store and Nicole approved it. The product images were uploaded and sizes marked available or sold out.

And then Nicole nodded to him to make it live.

He turned to her, finally, smiling. "Okay. We're live."

She nodded. "Okay."

"Don't worry. What's the worst thing that can happen?"

She could think of too many to pick just one but he said, "No one ever knows it's there and nothing happens."

"That's the worst thing you can think of?"

"Uh, yeah."

She shook her head, telling him to not sleep on his desk again tonight and she'd see him in the morning.

They'd see what the worst thing was tomorrow.

Because she was Nicole Bissette and no one ever knowing that it was there was never going to happen.

Fourteen

Nicole Bissette, daughter of famed supermodel Nikita, seems to be making a run for. . . something. She held her first NYFW runway only a few days ago and has now expanded her website to include an online store.

Yes, that's right. You, too, can own this season's ~~hottest newest~~ well, you can own one of this season's offerings.

If you hurry, because most items are marked "sold out".

Here's a hint to a ~~socialite~~ designer flailing around trying to find a place to plant her feet: next time have the store up before the runway.

Here's another hint: have product.

Meh. Seen palazzo pants before. I'm not paying $500 to wear Nicole Bissette's name on my ass.

hahahaha hahahaha hahahaha

Ugh, another wanna-be celebrity designer. Seriously, is there nothing else for them to do?

Fifteen

Nicole hid behind her desk, her head on her knees and her back digging into a drawer handle and her tears flowing rapidly down her cheeks.

Candy wrappers littered the floor next to her and she kept her eyes closed so she wouldn't have to see them.

She heard a knock on her door and ignored it like she'd ignored the half dozen before it, and then her eyes flew open when the door clicked open.

"Nicole?"

She stopped breathing, freezing at Flynn's voice.

The door closed again but she knew he'd come inside.

She swiped at her cheeks– should have worn waterproof mascara, she was going to look like a raccoon– and then he came around her desk.

He stopped and stared at her, his lips squeezing together.

She looked away, cleared her throat. She was going to tell him to go away and instead said, "I don't feel well."

He sat down cross-legged next to her.

He fiddled his thumbs.

He picked up a candy wrapper and twisted it in his

fingers.

Nicole said, "Gia said that candy makes everything better."

Flynn nodded and Nicole clutched her stomach.

"It doesn't."

"Ah."

"I'm going to vomit."

He made a grab for the wastebasket and shoved it under her chin just in time.

She retched and Flynn pulled her hair back, twisting it in his hand to keep it out of the way.

She coughed and spit and cried and when she was done, she lay down weakly on the carpet, pillowing her head on his thigh.

She moaned. "I think I'm going to OD on candy."

His hand stroked through her hair and Nicole closed her eyes.

He said, "I wonder if that's even possible."

"It feels like it. I don't think I'd mind too much."

"I can see the obituary now. Death by Tootsie Roll."

Nicole said, "Don't make me laugh."

"No? Crying's better?"

She nodded, her ear rubbing against his slacks and he shifted his leg.

They sat there in silence for a long minute, and then Flynn said softly, "What do they know? Really. What do they know?"

Nicole opened her eyes and stared at his cheap black dress shoes. And Darth Vader socks.

"You were right about prêt-à-porter. They called it port-a-pottay."

His legs shook under her ear and she pushed herself up. "Are you laughing?"

His held his breath, his face turning red, and he shook

his head with short, fast shakes.

She raised an eyebrow and he shook faster.

She turned until she was sitting next to him and thumped her back against the leg of the desk.

"It wasn't funny."

"It was kind of funny. Mean, but kind of funny. Maybe we should put a footnote underneath port-a-pottay that says, 'Listen, yo. She's French-American.'"

She laughed and then swiped at her nose with the back of her hand.

He reached above and behind him, searching for the box of Kleenex and pulling it down for her.

He said, "And maybe you should just consider everything they write about you as free advertising. I came in here to tell you that everything has sold out already."

She sniffed, wiping her eyes and nose with the Kleenex, and then took a deep breath. "Really?"

He lifted his eyebrows, trying not to grin like a fool.

She tried to smile but it wobbled. And she didn't know why that made her want to cry.

Flynn lifted his arm, putting it around her shoulders and giving her a friendly squeeze.

She grabbed another Kleenex. "I don't know why I'm crying *now*."

She put her head down on his shoulder and Flynn tried not to think about how good she smelled.

Much.

He cleared his throat quietly. "Want to watch a show? A good laugh will help."

"Will it?"

"It always makes me feel better."

"Okay." She sat up, turning around and propping her back against the wall of cupboards, and Flynn cursed at himself for being so damn stupid.

She said, "But if this turns out like the sugar thing, I'm going to fire you."

He pulled her laptop onto her chair, twisting it around so they could see and logged in to his account.

He sat down next to her, stretching out his legs.

"I've never puked after watching *The IT Crowd*. I think we're both okay."

Nicole covered her mouth quickly, like she'd just remembered. She glanced at the wastebasket, then jumped up to take it over to the door.

She tied the plastic bag up tight, then grabbed a water bottle from a desk drawer and swished and gargled.

She grabbed a piece of gum from her purse, then finally sat down again.

Flynn was sorry to say that she was farther away than she had been.

She said, embarrassed, "Sorry," and Flynn shrugged. All he'd been smelling the last few minutes had been vanilla.

Hey, it's really hard to notice anything when Nicole Bissette's head is in your lap.

They watched the first episode, Nicole relaxing as the canned track laughter made her stop thinking.

And the first time Roy said, "Have you tried turning it off and on again," Nicole looked at Flynn.

"You say that all the time."

"It fixes a lot of problems."

"Do you think it could fix me?"

"There's nothing to fix."

"I just ate *all that*." She waved her hand at all the wrappers still littering the floor.

"Seems like a normal amount. That's how much I ate last night for a bedtime snack."

She chuckled, thought about how she shouldn't, then chuckled again.

"Liar."

"I eat this much before dinner, as a warm-up."

"Then will you take the rest of it when you go?"

"Sure."

"You're going to eat it, aren't you?"

"Won't even make it to my closet."

She scooted closer, her shoulder resting lightly against his, and she sighed softly. "You make me laugh."

"I do?"

Nicole smiled at the screen and Flynn thought there was no shame in making a beautiful woman laugh. Especially when her eyes were still wet from her tears and her makeup had melted down her face.

She leaned against him, resting her head on his shoulder. "So which one are you? Roy or Moss?"

"Uhhh. . . Jen?"

Nicole laughed. "No."

"And you're the crazy boss who thinks I can build you a voice-activated computer."

She twisted her head up, seeing if he was joking, then smiled and snuggled back down.

"Could you?"

"Well, I could try. But probably not."

"I don't know. You did a really great job on the store. *They* said so."

"I don't know how to take that since we decided they didn't know anything. And they didn't really say anything about the design."

"Exactly. They would have skewered it if it hadn't been great."

He nodded, sighing. "Yeah. Me doing a good job means it's invisible."

She sniffed. "I'd give anything for invisibility."

"It is not all it's cracked up to be."

"Neither is fame."

That was probably true. But surely there was a happy medium between the two.

Nicole said softly, "First, they love you. Then, they hate you."

"No, they don't hate you. The ones who love you, still do. The ones who hate you are just the loudest right now."

She whispered, "It hurts. I know it shouldn't. But it hurts."

He sucked in a breath, then wrapped his arm around her and squeezed. Tight. Protecting her from invisible barbs, from unseen words.

As if he could.

She was stiff in his arms and he was berating himself for being a moron and crossing a line, definitely crossed a line there, and then, suddenly, she relaxed against him.

Her breath sighed out against his neck and her plain vanilla body wash wafted up and short-circuited his brain and her arm came around to wrap around his waist.

The screen froze for an instant, the movie buffering, and Nicole whispered, "It's not working."

She lifted her head slightly. Her face right there, her eyes looking into his, her mouth so close.

Don't kiss her. Don't kiss your boss.

And then, he remembered Hitch and was glad he'd watched it because he could go ninety percent. *Ninety percent of the way and hold.* With all women, but especially this one.

And if she didn't want to kiss him, she didn't have to.

He closed the difference between their lips by half and whispered back, "Have you tried turning it off and on again?"

She smiled. So slow, her lips pulling apart and her eyes crinkling. Her brown eyes melting into dark puddles.

Flynn's heart stopped beating and he forgot to breathe, and he whispered, "Your eyes are the color of a Tootsie Roll."

She blinked, wrinkled her forehead, and sat back.

"A Tootsie Roll?"

He let her go, grabbing a handful of candy and picking out one to compare. He held it up next to her face.

"Yep, a Tootsie Roll."

"Could you have at least picked *real* chocolate? Godiva? Ghirardelli? A *Tootsie Roll*?"

"I like Tootsie Rolls."

"It's chocolate *flavor*. You could have said I was 70% cacao. Rich, warm, smooth, intense."

"No, I couldn't have said that. That's not anything I would have ever said."

"A Tootsie Roll!"

She sounded so sincerely offended he just leaned forward and kissed her. Forgot about ninety percent, forgot about waiting, forgot that she was Nicole Bissette.

Just kissed her, his lips lightly touching hers. His eyes open and staring into hers. His hand reaching for hers.

She murmured, "I just threw up."

He murmured back, "I'm going to have to tell you that I would put up with a lot to kiss you. Mint gum with hints of puke don't really rate."

She tried not to laugh but she did. And she pulled her lips from his but held on to his hand. "You're disgusting."

He shrugged. "All men are."

"And you think I'm a Tootsie Roll."

He laughed, saying, "It wasn't an insult," and she looked at him pointedly.

"And all I said was that your eyes were the *color* of a Tootsie Roll. That's not what I think you *are*."

"Mm-hm."

"I think you are a goddess with Tootsie Roll colored eyes."

She didn't say anything to that, just looked at him, and he wondered what she could see with those Tootsie Roll colored eyes.

She said softly, "I think you're Clark Kent. Superman in disguise."

He blinked. "Superman? I think I love you."

She laughed. "I was going to say Superman in a boring tie but changed my mind."

"Oh, well, you know." He looked down at his plain old black tie. "Boring is the new black, I guess."

She smiled again and he said, "Yeah, you're right. You should put that thing away."

She didn't.

Just smiled at him, looking. Watching. Waiting.

This wasn't Resting Bitch Face.

This was *Don't stop* and *Yes* and *You're welcome*.

He leaned toward her again and Nicole whispered, "What about Lois Lane?"

Flynn ran his fingers through her hair and Nicole slid her hand underneath his suit jacket and he said, "She'll get over it."

Sixteen

Nicole Bissette thinks I'm Superman.

Yep. Totally not what he would have guessed she was thinking about him.

And even more unbelievable, *he'd just made out with Nicole Bissette.*

Like, that was something that should be shared with bros.

Except, it hadn't been Nicole Bissette smiling at him. She didn't smile.

It had been Nicole.

Smiling at him and him alone.

So he told no one, and he just went home again.

Let his mom fix him food and let his Dad talk him into fixing the computer. Again.

And when Flynn did it without lecturing about clicking on strange links just because *YOU'VE WON*, Mike said, "You okay, Flynn?"

Flynn nodded. "I just. . .met a girl."

His dad turned toward the door and yelled, "Lisa!"

When she poked her head into the room, Mike said, "He met a girl."

His mom came all the way in, wiping her hands on a dish towel and trying not to be overexcited.

"Ohh! What's she like?"

Flynn stared at the screen and typed. "She's a ten."

"Out of your league," Mike said, lightly punching his son's shoulder. "Good for you."

"Mike! That's not out of his league."

Flynn and Mike exchanged a look, and Flynn wobbled his hand back and forth. "A three?"

"At least a three and a half. Maybe a four."

They both smiled when Lisa gripped his face, tipping it to the light.

"You're an eight, if not a nine."

"Mom, I think you're biased."

"I am not. Tell him, Mike."

"Maybe a five. In the right light."

Lisa glared at her husband, dropping Flynn's face. "*You're* a five."

Mike laughed. "So, come on. Tell us about this girl."

Flynn sighed and paused, staring at his fingers on the keyboard.

"I like her. And she's out of my league. That's pretty much it."

"Well. Maybe she's like your mom and thinks you're a nine. She like you back?"

"For a little while."

Lisa said, "What does that mean?"

"It means our son is playing the field," Mike said and sniffed with pride.

Flynn snorted. "Yes. I'm an eight or a nine and instead of being played, am doing the playing."

Mike stopped smiling. "She's just playing with you?"

"I don't know what she's doing with me."

"Is she a player?"

Flynn shook his head.

"Then maybe she can see inside you, where you're a ten."

"Aww." Lisa smiled at her husband. "And that's what bumps you from a five to a five and three-quarters."

Flynn didn't know what Nicole was doing with him but she really wasn't a player. Maybe she did see something inside him. She had said she thought he was Superman.

Mike grabbed Lisa, pulling her onto his lap. "I'll give you a five and three-quarters."

Flynn grimaced and said, "You want me to fix this computer or not?"

"I'd rather kiss your mom."

"Okey-dokey. Going upstairs."

Lisa stayed on her husband's lap, listening to the soft tread of her youngest son as he went up the stairs, and said, "It's Nicole Bissette."

"What?!" Mike shook his head. "Nah. She's not a ten."

"Your gauge is broken."

"Really? 'Cause I would have said you were a ten."

"Aww." She turned, putting her arms around his neck. "You can kiss me now."

"Only if you bump me up to a six."

She gripped his face between her hands. "You're an eight, if not a nine. But if that gets out, I'll be chasing other women away all day long and never have time to cook your dinner."

He thought about it, then nodded. "That works for me."

Seventeen

Nicole went home, too.

Not because she'd had the worst/best day of her life.

Not because she'd cried her eyes out, her spirit twisting under the knife of ugly words. Not because Flynn had come in and made her laugh. Had held her and kissed her and made her feel like a goddess.

Nicole laughed.

A goddess.

With Tootsie Roll colored eyes.

She knew she wasn't because the real goddess was laying on the sofa, the skin on her face raw, red, and chunky from her chemical peel.

Nikita took one look at her daughter and said, "And why have you spent the day crying your eyes out? They're all red and puffy."

Nicole sat stiffly in an armchair. "I wanted to know what people thought of the store."

Nikita sighed, closing her eyes. "You have skin as thin as tissue paper. Who cares what people *think*; it only matters what they *do*."

"What did you think of it?"

And *this* is why she had come home. For the truth.

No Gia to hold her, so she turned to Flynn.

No Victoria for the truth, so she turned to her mother.

"I think that you were sold out when I looked at it."

"Yes."

"So, well done, darling."

Nicole sat back in her chair, silent, and Nikita said, "The results are all that matter. Everything else is an opinion, and everyone has one."

Nicole whispered, "How do you not care?"

Her mother's mouth opened for a frozen, pain-filled chortle.

"I do it with a massive ego. *My* opinion is the only opinion I care about. What did *you* think about it?"

"I don't know."

"You'll never be free of other people's opinion, Nicole, until you learn to listen, and trust, your own."

"It's really hard to take your platitudes seriously when you're lying here bleeding onto your sofa because you can't stand the fact that you're aging."

Nikita opened her eyes to glare at her daughter. "Then move the towel to where it needs to be, Nicole."

When the towel was moved, Nikita cleared her throat. "I needed a touchup. And that was *my* opinion after seeing photos of me at various shows this last week." She gingerly patted the skin on her cheek and muttered, "Should have done it weeks before."

"Me, too. Not the face, the store. Should have had it up before the show. Should have had more product."

Nikita waved a hand. "In the past. You can't know what you don't know until you know it. And more importantly, unchangeable." She smiled at her daughter with her eyes. "We'll both do better next year."

"I don't. . . I don't think I'll do another runway. I know

now that I didn't enjoy it."

"But darling, you have such flair! I should have put you in acting classes. Got you out of your own skin."

"Well, this has been lovely. I'll leave now, before we both ruin it."

Nikita held her hands up in surrender, sighing out a deep breath.

"Stay, at least until Nicolette gets home."

Nicole lifted her eyebrows. "And when will that be?"

"Not long. It will surprise you to learn that she enjoys being at home."

"It doesn't surprise me at all, when you don't care that she has a boyfriend eight years older than she is. When you do nothing about the cocaine."

"It's part of our world, Nicole."

"It's not a good part."

Nikita shrugged. So Gallic, so dismissive.

"Mother."

Nikita frowned at her. "Nicole. Really. You know I don't like that word."

"That's what you are, Nikita. A mother. To a seventeen-year-old girl who needs you to be one."

"When I was seventeen, I was on my own. And I had boyfriends who were eight years older. And I had the coke, too."

"And you turned out fine," Nicole said sarcastically. "You had a child when you were eighteen! Is that what you want for her?"

Nikita snorted softly, then flinched in pain. She sat up slowly, trying not to jar her face. "I don't want anything for my Nicolette, I'll let her want for herself. Just like I did for you."

"You let me? Oh yes, thank you for not being a mother to me. For not giving me a father. For letting me figure it all out on my own."

"You're welcome," her mother said, and Nicole's throat burned with the effort it took not to scream at her.

"My parents had my life all figured out for me and they were wrong." Nikita held her arms up, indicating the loft. "Look what I have. Look what I've done for myself. Look where *my* want has taken me.

"We don't know where your want will take you yet, do we? That's a gift, Nicole. We don't know where Nicolette's want will take her. Although I'm afraid that if I want Nicolette to move out, I'll have to kick her out. Most likely when she's forty. But I don't mind her staying. My oldest daughter left when she was fourteen and never came back. It was too soon."

"I went to school."

"Is that what you tell yourself? You may have left *properly*, finding yourself an environment that felt like you hadn't just ripped yourself away from your home, but you left just as surely as I did. You're more like me than you want to admit."

Nikita raised an eyebrow at the look of horror on her daughter's face.

"My drive. My ambition." She waved her hand in the air. "Nicolette takes after her father. Happy to let the current take her where it will."

Nicole wouldn't ask, because it didn't matter. Not now, when she was twenty-seven.

It was too late.

So she didn't know why she said, "Did he know about me? My father?"

"Yes. But he was married, so that complicated things. He still is, surprisingly enough. I suppose some women are too much of a bitch to ever divorce. A man's secrets, and all his money, would go with her when she left." Nikita chuckled. "That's probably why I never married. It would be for forever."

She studied Nicole's pale face for a long minute. "Well? Are you going to ask me who? I always figured you would ask when you needed to know. Nicolette asked me when she was ten. But where angels fear to tread, there goes my Nicolette."

"It doesn't matter. He obviously didn't care enough about me to ever bother introducing himself."

"Well, he did set up a very nice trust fund for you. Sometimes it is all a parent can do."

That was a shock and Nicole sat there, knowing her mother had just given her the key to her father's identity. She could just go look at the papers.

She said, hesitantly, "Do I know him?"

"Yes."

Nicole took in a deep breath and shook her head. She didn't want to find out here, not with Nikita watching for her reaction.

Nikita said, "I won't tell you unless you ask. Sometimes it is all a parent can do."

Nicole snorted and stood. "All you can do is nothing? I'm shocked."

"I won't tell and you won't ask. Not like me at all, hmm?"

"No, I'm not."

Nikita adjusted the towel and lay back down. "Must be why we get along so well."

Nicole left, and she did not slam the door on the way out.

Sometimes it was all a daughter could do.

Eighteen

Flynn was kicked back in his chair, his feet up on his metal desk, when Nicole flung open his closet door and ran in, shutting the door smoothly behind her.

"What are–"

She waved at him wildly to stop talking, taking two big steps to press her finger against his lips.

"Shh. My mother is here."

Her father, too. Dammit, she should have never brought it up with Nikita.

Shouldn't have looked at the trust papers.

Should have gone on, happily blissful, without ever knowing.

Except she'd never been happily blissful.

She'd never been happy.

And she did know him, had known him since before she could even remember.

It had been almost too much to hope that she'd be happy with who her father was but despite the fact that he was nearly twenty years older than her mother– oh yes, and married– she was happy.

. . .happy-ish. Not unhappy, at least.

Nicole looked at the finger still pressed to Flynn's lips and whispered, "Sorry."

All morning she'd wondered what she'd say to him when she saw him again.

After yesterday.

She'd thought it would be awkward. She'd decided she would just avoid him all day.

I mean, what do you say to a guy the day after you eat a mountain of candy, vomit, and then make out with him?

But it had all been shoved under the panic of seeing and knowing her father. Of knowing that her whole life she could have known, if she'd only looked.

Maybe she hadn't wanted to know. Maybe she hadn't wanted to look.

She could have asked Nikita at any time, and hadn't.

Flynn mumbled, "Not going to lie. I don't hate this," and Nicole's panic receded. And the awkwardness just wasn't there.

She took her finger off his lips and he looked at her gaping shirt, at a peek of dark purple lace, and he gasped.

Nicole tsked. "Terrible design. Not my own obviously."

Flynn swallowed. "I appreciate a poor design on the odd occasion."

"I can't have it be said that I don't pay my debts," she said, and he stopped looking down her shirt long enough to laugh into her eyes.

Her lips pressed together, and then she remembered where she was. In a windowless closet with Flynn, so she smiled back because no one could see her but him. She put her lips against his and wrapped her arms around his neck and said, "I don't hate this either."

Off went her cardigan, and Nicole briefly understood why women wore shirts that gaped open.

Sometimes you *did* want to show off your bra.

And then her blouse disappeared, and Flynn's tie was flung out carelessly behind her.

He stood, hoisting her up onto his desk and then cupping dark purple lace gently. He stared at his hands, taking a deep breath.

"You smell so good."

"It's vanilla. Plain vanilla. That's all that I am."

She pulled back, looking at him, hoping he would understand. She was just plain vanilla.

He watched her for a long moment, then shook his head. "Just say it. Stop *looking* at me and just say whatever it is you're thinking."

I'm just plain vanilla. Want me anyway.

But he couldn't read her mind, no one could, and she whispered, "*Please.*"

His eyes widened and he said with reverence, "My lady. I am yours."

Nineteen

Their feet were under the corner of Flynn's desk, and his head was wedged in the opposite corner of the tiny room. Nicole's head was tucked under his chin and her arm across his chest.

Flynn couldn't help it, he swore allegiance to the god of morning nookie with a lopsided grin on his face. "I will put gel in my hair every morning."

Nicole pushed up to look. "I didn't even notice."

"Must have been subliminal."

She touched a crunchy lock. "Probably not. I was just distracted."

"Bad distracted or good distracted?"

"Bad distracted. Then good distracted."

"That's horribly honest of you," he said but he remembered how she had begged him.

She had begged *him*.

Nicole smoothed a hand across his chest. "You weren't any part of the bad distracted."

"Thank you."

"And I'll fix your hair for you."

"Thank you."

She lay back down again, and Flynn let out a long, satisfied smile. That faltered a little when he noticed how close his head was to the door.

"I really hope no one needs their phone fixed."

Nicole's head rubbed against his chest as she looked at the door. "Is there a lock?"

"There's not usually a lock on the inside of a closet. I'm only vaguely worried that one day I'm going to get locked in from the outside." He grinned. "I've got snacks in the bottom drawer just in case it happens."

"Snacks?"

"I like to be prepared."

"We could probably take the lock off."

"Or put one on the inside? Might come in useful," he said with naked boss in his arms.

"I had a lock on the inside of my closet when I was growing up."

Flynn pondered that. "I'm trying to come up with a good reason why. You had an office when you were a kid?"

Her breath puffed against his skin. "No. It was my hidey-hole. To keep me and my sister safe during parties."

Flynn didn't know what to say to that but he could feel her heart thumping against him.

He said softly, "Nikita must have thrown some real ragers, huh?"

She shifted and his arms tightened reflexively. "You don't have to tell me."

Nicole let out a quiet breath. "You can probably guess the kind of parties drugged-out supermodels throw. She was only eighteen when she had me. By the time Colette was born, she'd outgrown them somewhat. She's ragingly respectable now in comparison."

"Still scary."

He felt her smile. "Yes. But I had my sanctuary when I

needed it."

Flynn lifted his head up, scanning his walls. "I can totally see sanctuary. Cozy. Cloistered. Tell me you had a lot of books in there with you."

"Mm, some. Lots of fashion magazines. And a TV."

He turned his head to stare at her in disbelief. "You had a *TV* in your *closet*?"

"It wasn't a *small* closet."

"Are you telling me your clothes closet growing up was bigger than my office closet is now?"

She turned her head, calculating dimensions. "Umm. . . No, I'm not going to tell you that."

His head flopped back onto the floor and she squeezed him. "I already asked if you wanted a bigger office."

"I'm changing my answer."

"You can if you want but I'm liking this."

Flynn was liking it, too. A lot.

And he liked it even more when she asked, "Can I stay with you in your small closet for a while?"

Flynn's heart started racing and he wondered if she could feel it.

But then he remembered.

"Nikita is probably still out there, huh?" He took a gulp of breath and went as falsetto as he could and opera-ed, "*Sanctuary!*"

Nicole laughed against his side, bobbing against him so hard he thought she might break.

Nothing wrong with the world when you're lying on the floor naked with a laughing, *naked*, woman beside you.

She sighed her breath out and when he glanced down at her, her smile was so wide and beautiful and heart stoppingly open, he just forgot. . .everything.

Just watched her.

He felt a tingle down by his toes but was still looking at

Nicole so promptly forgot about it.

She said, "You make me laugh."

"I *try* to make you laugh. Every once in a while I get you to break."

She laughed at him again. "Thank you for granting me sanctuary."

"Of course. I won't even take it personally because it's Nikita. But you've got to sing it."

"You could probably take it a little personally, but my father is here with her." She shook her head at him. "And, nope."

"Dad, too? Right, we're going to be here a while. We can watch *The Hunchback of Notre Dame*." He opened his arms as wide as he could. "*Sanctuary!*"

"It's never, not ever, going to happen. And I don't like Hunchback."

"Too much fiery hellfire? Too many faceless demons?"

"Yes."

Flynn thought about the demon waiting somewhere in the office for Nicole and understood completely.

"Are you tired of *The IT Crowd* yet?"

She smiled up at him. "No. Not tired of the I.T. crowd at all."

He thought about getting up and getting his laptop but, had he mentioned, there was a naked *smiling* woman in his arms?

He reluctantly said, "I hate to say this, I *really* hate to say this, but maybe we should get dressed. Someone's going to need something from me sooner or later."

"A tablet to turn off and on again?"

Tingle.

"Yes!" Flynn tried a bored monotone Irish accent. "*Have you tried turning it off and on again?*"

She laughed, using his chest to push herself up. "Does

your boss know you sit in here watching shows all day?"

"She does now."

She found her skirt and shook it out. Handed him his pants with a resigned sigh. "I should tell her you don't have enough to do."

"We're working on it."

"I do have some ideas about that."

He looked at her eagerly, stuffing his arms in his shirt. "Oh, yeah?"

"Not right now, though. Maybe we can talk about it during lunch."

Flynn grinned. "Does your boss know you work through lunch?"

"My boss thinks that's what lunch is for."

She pulled on her cardigan, and looked at his hair.

"We might need to go to my office to fix it," she began and the closet door swung open.

Nikita looked between them briefly, then stepped inside the suddenly overcrowded room and shut the door.

"Nicole, really. If you can't help but dally with your staff, put a boa on the doorknob."

She untied the intricately wrapped scarf from around her hair and chin and took off her oversized sunglasses and Flynn met the demon eyes of Nikita Bissette.

"*Jesus Christ,*" he screamed and fell into his chair.

Nicole threw Flynn's tie at him and said soothingly, "It's a chemical peel."

Flynn couldn't look away. "It looks like hamburger."

"It heals. And takes years off."

Flynn didn't doubt it since it had taken years off *his* life.

Not to mention he'd never be able to look at raw hamburger again.

Nikita looked him up and down slowly, her mouth pulling back into a hideous grimace by the time her eyes reached his black socks.

She said, "Well."

Flynn opened his mouth, to say what he didn't know, but he met Nikita's eyes again and decided he'd just sit here quietly and finish tying his tie.

"Mother," Nicole said, and Nikita's head whipped toward her. "What are you doing out and about before you're healed?"

Nikita blew out a breath. "I called my old friend James Geary this morning, and he said he'd take me to a discreet place for lunch. I was just *dying* to get out, so took him up on the offer. I thought you might like to join us? It's been forever since he's seen you as well."

Nicole said nothing, just stared at her mother, and Nikita's lips curled up.

"That didn't take you long, did it?"

Flynn shivered a little at the smile but Nicole remained unmoved.

"No, it didn't."

"Come to lunch with us," Nikita said, making Flynn think of hamburgers.

Nicole began crowding her mother toward the door. "No, thank you."

Nikita raised an eyebrow. "That's it? No, thank you?"

Nicole reached around her and turned the knob. "That's it."

"Don't be rude, Nicole. He's taken time out of his busy day to see you."

Nicole raised *her* eyebrow, and Flynn thought there should be yellow subtitles underneath their eyebrows.

Nikita: *I challenge you*!

Nicole: *To the death*!

A showdown right here in his little closet.

And then he remembered that some innocent bystander

was always skewered through the middle in these kinds of showdowns, and since he was the only one here. . .

He gulped and said, "We already made lunch plans. Sorry, Nikita. Maybe next time?"

Twenty

Nicole took Flynn to sushi. And picked out all her favorites for him to try.

It took too much effort to remember not to smile at him. Out here where others could see as well.

And he tried so hard to get her to break.

Making jokes and overreacting after tasting the *nigiri*, and finally, making her laugh silently into her napkin, her shoulders shaking and tears streaming.

She said, finally, "Damn you."

But it was without heat, and he grinned at her, taking a too-big bite of pickled ginger.

And then his eyes were streaming as well and he was crying into his napkin.

She was still laughing when she looked up into the eyes of her father.

"Nicole."

Resting Bitch Face snapped back into place, and she said, "Mr. Geary."

He nodded slowly, looking away for a quick moment.

Then he met her eyes again. "I thought you knew."

"I didn't."

"I can see that. Now." He indicated the chair opposite her. "May I?"

Nicole glanced at Flynn, then nodded. "This is my. . ."

Flynn raised both eyebrows. "Lacky? Grunt?"

Nicole bit her lip to keep from smiling. "IT Specialist."

Mr. Geary nodded absently, and when the silence stretched on and on, said, "I didn't think this would be awkward. We know each other."

Flynn mouthed, *I'm gonna go*, and Nicole shook her head at him with tiny jerky movements.

Mr. Geary cleared his throat. "We're having a family dinner tonight. I would love if you would come."

"What about your wife?"

"She knows. She's always known. And you can meet my son, Scott."

Nicole blinked, remembering Scott Geary. Her brother, now.

"I have met him."

New York might be a metropolitan but her social circles were small.

"Meet him as your brother."

The silence stretched on and on again, and Nicole said, "It's funny that you didn't think this would be awkward, Mr. Geary."

"Funny is one word for it. And you can call me James. Or Father."

She replied dryly, "I always wondered where I got my sense of humor from."

"Come tonight and find out what else you got from me." He didn't wait for the silence this time, just said, "It's your choice. It's always been your choice."

She looked at him with dry humor shining from her eyes.

His lips twitched. "Giving you a choice may not have

been the right thing to do when you were a child. It's the only way we can go forward now." He stood. "I would like to go forward. You'll have to decide what you want."

James Geary handed her his card. "I hope I'll see you tonight."

He nodded at Flynn, then turned away.

Nicole watched him walk away and, yes, she was wondering what else she'd got from him.

Her humor, maybe. Her trust fund, definitely.

Like it or not, he *was* her father.

And she had a brother.

Suddenly, she was intimately connected to twice as many people as before.

She looked at Flynn, who was looking at a glob of wasabi at the end of his chopstick.

She opened her mouth to warn him, and then she closed it.

And then she waited for him to chase away the last awkward silence.

Twenty-One

Nicole decided to go to dinner.

And then decided not to.

Yes, no, yes.

She almost asked Flynn to come with her, but at the last minute changed her mind. Not only had he not been invited, she wasn't at all sure she wanted him to see her being introduced to her *other* family.

She had called Victoria for a bracing pick-me-up, alongside the news about just who her father and new brother were, but there had been no answer. Too busy getting her newest project into shipshape.

So she called Gia for a not-so-bracing pep talk.

They had been her first *other* family, and Nicole smiled when Gia's grandmother was the one to answer the phone.

She'd heard enough stories of the older woman to know that Gia loved her dearly. And that the woman was cra-zy.

Nonna asked, "Are you the too-skinny one?"

"Umm. . ."

"The one who won't smile?"

"Oh, yes. That's me."

"A woman is always prettier when she is smiling."

"Yes."

Nonna hummed in the back of her throat. "Beauty. She is a two-edged sword."

"Yes."

"Your other friend uses hers as a weapon."

Nicole looked at the phone. "Have you met Victoria?"

"I hear stories. But *your* beauty has cut too many times and you are afraid of it."

". . .can I talk to Gia?"

Nonna ignored the request and said, "It's nice and warm here."

"Okay."

"Gia says it was dog cold in New York when she left."

Nicole looked at the phone again, then said, "Still is."

"I was sad to say goodbye to New York but I do not miss the cold. Gia will like it here when she stops crying about her hair."

Nicole thought that Nonna was probably right and said softly, "I hope she finds what she's looking for there."

"A man! That's what she's looking for. Babies! That's what she needs."

"Okay. Can I talk to Gia?"

Nonna hacked a laugh, then yelled right into the phone, "Gia! It's your friend from New York!"

Nicole jerked her ear away from the phone, giving herself a crick in the neck, and she said, "Ow."

There was a scuffle and a change of hands and Nicole heard a faint, "*Nonnie, don't answer my phone.*"

"*It was ringing.*"

Gia sighed, and then said into the phone, "She's trying to catch Mac."

"*Mia creatura, I'm seventy-three years old. Time is a-ticking.*"

"*Then probably you should focus on someone else. Not

him."

Nicole said, "Who's Mac?"

"Someone I do not want to talk about because I spend all day shopping for him, and then I spend all evening arguing with him about what I spent all day shopping for."

"Fashion consultant is going well then?"

"Gah! I'm ripping out my hair."

"Just remember you can always come back and work for me."

"I might be tempted to if I wasn't still stinging over you calling me plus-sized."

"What did she call you?! I curse her! Evil eye! Malocchio! I spit on her! Spit!"

"No, Nonnie! She's my friend. She apologized already!"

"All of her hair will fall out! Tell her I'm doing evil eye at her."

"You know evil eye only works in person, not over the phone."

"I send a picture. Give me phone."

"No! Mom, help!"

Click.

Nicole massaged her neck, and a minute later, Gia called back. "Can't talk long, I'm hiding in the bathroom."

"It was a technical term. And I am sorry."

"I know. And I'm sorry if all your hair falls out."

Nicole said, "I'll let you know. Have you talked to Victoria?"

Gia laughed. "Yeah. And if you think I sound like I want to commit murder, you should hear her."

"You two should never have left New York."

"We deserve everything we get. What about you? Things okay?"

"Yes."

Gia waited.

Nicole said, "Some good. Some bad."

Gia waited.

"I ate a lot of candy and then vomited in front of Flynn."

"I hope that was the bad."

Nicole said, "Yes. I-met-my-father-and-I-kissed-Flynn."

Gia didn't even have to take a minute to translate.

"Want to talk about the bad first or the good?"

"I don't want to talk about the bad. Yet."

"Okay, then yes! Tell me the kiss was good."

Nicole closed her eyes, remembering, then finally said, "He might have kissed me. I can't remember which. But, yes, it *is* good. I slept with him."

"Should have led with that!"

"It would have sounded slutty to say I slept with him first. I kissed him, and then I slept with him. In that order."

Gia laughed. "Okay. Glad we're clear on that."

"He was flippant with Nikita."

Gia sighed. "Oh. . .man. . . I had high hopes for Flynn. When's his funeral?"

"I think she must be taking Valium, Xanax, something. He's still standing."

"I have very high hopes for Flynn."

Nicole smiled, refusing to think about her hopes for Flynn. She was just having a little bit, a lotta bit, of fun with him. And fun was a new and. . .fun. . .experience for her.

So she just said, "Yeah."

"You ready to talk about the bad yet?"

"No. I just wanted to talk to someone who loves me."

"I love you and I will always have your back."

Nicole swallowed the lump in her throat. "I know. I love you and I will always have your back, too, even if it's in Florida."

It might not have meant the same to Gia. She had dozens, multiple dozens, of family who loved her and always had her back. But one more surely couldn't hurt.

Gia must have known that Nicole had got what she needed because she said, "Okay then. Good talk. Want to hear about this *testa di cazzo* I'm working for?"

Nicole smiled and leaned back in her chair. "I really, really do."

Twenty-Two

James Geary was pleased to see her when she was shown in to dinner.

He stood, gripping her shoulders and smiling, and Nicole thought for a moment that he was going to hug her. But at the last minute he simply kissed her cheek and then turned to introduce her to people she already knew.

"You know my wife, of course. Cornelia Geary."

They nodded at each other, Nicole looking for signs of. . .hate? Welcome?

What does a woman feel when her husband's long lost child finally shows up?

Because Nicole remembered her mother saying, *Some women are too much of a bitch to ever divorce.*

Though, perhaps the *other woman* wasn't the best judge of a man's wife.

And Nicole remembered James saying, *My wife knows. She's always known.*

But Cornelia only stood to kiss her cheek and murmur, "It happened a long time ago."

"Yes."

"Time, perhaps, for this secret to see the light of day."

Nicole's stomach turned. Scandal and secrets.

Well, *this* time, she wouldn't look at the comments.

Cornelia said, "We should have a consistent story, at least."

James pulled out a chair for Nicole. "Yes, but not now. Later. There'll be lots of time for that, later."

"Of course, dear."

The women had nothing more to say to each other, then, and Nicole turned to the other man in the room.

Her brother.

Scott had stood at her entrance, and he held out his hand to her in greeting before they all sat down for their first family dinner.

And she could see in his eyes exactly what she felt. The trying to switch from acquaintance to family.

He said to her, "Imagine if *we'd* dated."

"Nightmare."

He grinned. "I won't take that comment personally. Drink?"

Dear God, yes, but she merely said, "Wine would be nice."

James frowned as Scott poured her a glass. "I would have made sure you two wouldn't have accidentally dated."

Scott grunted. "Sure. Because you've known about all the women I've dated." He pointed at Nicole. "I was damn near engaged to her best friend and you never said a word."

"You were dating her best friend, not her," James said and Nicole agreed.

"It did ensure we would never accidentally date."

Scott took a long drink. "I wonder how that break-up would have gone if we'd known about *this*."

Nicole said loyally, "She's my best friend."

"And I'm your brother." Scott opened his eyes maniacally wide. "Who you going to choose, sis?"

They grinned at each other, one tiny knot in her stomach loosening a smidgen, and she said, "I've known her longer."

"And she's scarier."

Nicole said, "It will probably be better if you don't date any more of my friends."

"Oh, I'm not dating anyone, ever again. I'm just waiting for more sisters to come out of the woodwork," Scott said, and then they both paused.

They turned to look at James at the same time.

He closed his eyes and blew out his lips. "None that I know of."

Scott said dryly, "Comforting."

Nicole couldn't help it. She sniggered.

Scott took another long sip. "Perhaps you should give up dating as well, Nicole. Sisters. Brothers. There may very well be legions of them."

Nicole glanced at James. Her until now unknown father.

He said, "There isn't."

Nicole looked down at her still empty plate. She looked up at her brother, his one eyebrow cocked in disbelief.

And she thought, for the first time, that this was her second chance. For a family. To be someone else and not just the daughter of.

Not just the daughter of her famous mother. Not just the daughter of James Geary.

But to be Nicole Bissette, whoever that turned out to be.

So she opened her mouth and said, "Well, I'm reassured."

Scott laughed, sloshing his drink and putting it down hastily.

Cornelia sighed. "I am so very glad both of you inherited your father's sense of humor."

James smiled at his wife. And then his son. And then his daughter.

And perhaps she *had* inherited his sense of humor because Nicole smiled back and said, "Me, too."

Twenty-Three

Nicole waited until she got home to try Victoria again.

The phone rang and rang. Nicole's chin wobbled with every ring and she needed a bracing pep talk from her best friend and why wouldn't she answer the phone?

"Nicole?"

"Yes?"

". . .I was going to tell you I'll call you later. Why are you crying?"

"I'm not crying. I'm thinking about crying."

"Keep thinking about it. I'll call you back in five minutes."

"Okay."

So she thought about crying, and why she wanted to cry. She'd had a nice dinner. It had been very nice. It had been awkward, and then not awkward.

Certainly not family, not yet.

But they'd had a nice dinner together.

And it made her want to cry!

She'd been prepared for bad, been expecting bad. Bad wouldn't have fazed her!

Nicole answered her phone on the first ring and

Victoria said, "Okay, I'm in what constitutes an office in this madhouse run by a moron. Why are you crying?"

"I met my father."

"Oh. Who is it?"

"James Geary."

"James Geary? Wait, *Scott Geary* James Geary.

"Yes."

Victoria barked out a laugh. And then another.

"I'm sorry. No wait, I need to do that a few more times."

Nicole listened to Victoria laughing and stopped thinking about crying. She found a box of Kleenex and patted her cheeks dry.

Victoria came back on the phone. "Sometimes, I really do think there is a God and He's just up there snacking on bonbons while watching this soap opera."

"Scott says hello," Nicole said and Victoria laughed again.

"No, he doesn't."

"No, he doesn't. But I told him I've known you longer and I choose you."

"Good. . . Scott Geary is your brother. That's going to take a little while to sink in."

"He wanted to marry you."

"LOL," Victoria said with no humor in her voice. "And HWACD."

"I don't. . ."

"He Was A Cheating Dickbag."

Nicole nodded her head and looked out the window at nighttime city lights. And felt the first flutterings of loyalty toward her new family.

"But your father would say anything to stop you from doing something he thought was stupid. And you said that Scott never admitted it."

Victoria's father would say and do anything to get what he wanted. Or he would have. The Alzheimer's was eating away all he had been more every day.

Victoria's tone was a tad frosty when she asked, "Did you ask Scott about it when he didn't say hello?"

"We steered the conversation to other subjects."

"My side, remember?"

"Yes. And I am. But I sat across from Scott tonight and liked him."

Victoria whispered, "I liked him, too."

Nicole knew. Victoria would have married him. And Nicole knew that Victoria had been devastated after their as-far-from-amicable-as-you-can-possibly-get-without-anyone-actually-dying breakup.

Nicole said, "Okay, so this is going to be awkward. No getting around that."

"No getting around it. Will our friendship survive?"

"Don't even joke about that."

Nicole could hear the beauty queen smile coming back into her friend's voice as Victoria said, "I won't joke about that, then. But if we're still friends, we'll need to talk about how you slept with Flynn."

"So, you'll give Gia non-crying minutes but not me?"

"She texted me the news. It said, 'Nicole. Flynn. Slap-slap. Yay!'"

Nicole closed her eyes. "Don't even joke about that."

"Sadly, I am not. Is it still going well with him?"

"It was just this morning."

"And? Is it still going well? Remember I'm on retainer if you need *his balls ripped off*."

"O-kay. You said that more vehemently than I was expecting."

Victoria chipped out, "A moron just stepped into my *office*. I was talking to the both of you."

A deep male voice muttered in the background, sounding not at all scared of getting his balls ripped off.

Victoria pulled the phone away and all Nicole could hear was sarcasm dripping from her friend's tongue like acid.

Then Victoria said more clearly, "I'll wait."

Nicole looked at the phone. "Are you talking to me?"

"No. Okay, now I'm talking to you. The moron has left the room."

"I'm so glad you're my friend," Nicole said, because she'd have to move to a different continent if they were enemies.

"Me, too. Even if you're related to Scott Geary."

"Nope. Let's not do that."

Victoria blew out a breath. "Okay. I'm sorry. I won't take my irritation out on you."

"Do you want to talk about him?"

"I thought we were done talking about Scott Geary."

Nicole smiled a little smile. "Not him."

There was a long pause and then Victoria said incredulously, "Do I want to talk about *the moron*? No. He's a moron. Quite possibly the dumbest person alive."

"Working in a startup in San Francisco?"

"Yes, that kind of dumb. He wears low tops like he's in high school still. Sometimes, if it's not raining, he switches it up with open-toed sandals. With socks."

"Sandals with socks. Is that a thing in San Francisco?"

Victoria sighed. "He is apparently originally from Oregon. And refuses to evolve, even to San Francisco levels. Like I said, moron."

"Working in a startup in San Francisco."

"He's a dumb, brilliant moron."

"You'll fix him right up, I have no doubt."

"Oh, he can't be fixed. His business on the other

hand. . .is still a maybe. And that means I need to get back. You done crying?"

Bracing. It's what Nicole had needed.

She'd confessed her familial sins. Could, perhaps, enjoy that she'd liked her new family.

Wanted to like her new family.

Didn't mean she was betraying her other families.

Either of them.

But it sure was getting complicated.

Twenty-Four

Three hours later, Nicole was woken by the buzzing of her phone and a very up close and personal picture of one evil eye.

An Italian grandmother's version of *I love you and I will always have your back.*

Twenty-Five

Flynn made it to work early the next day. Rage pumping through his veins, he'd practically run the entire way, paper fisted in his hand.

Nicole smiled when she saw him rush into her office and it made him pause, just a slight check, before he blurted, "I'm sorry I made you cry."

She cocked her head. "When?"

"Yesterday at lunch."

"You mean when you made me laugh so hard I cried?"

"Yes."

"Um, apology not accepted. I had a good time."

"It doesn't look like it in the pictures."

He threw the rumpled paper on her desk. Not at her, just away from himself, and she said, "Ah. Flynn don't read what they write. It's just a story. I myself have recommitted to not looking at what others write about me."

"They make it sound like I was yelling at you, making you cry." He'd been there, *knew* that wasn't what happened, and the pictures still made his stomach turn.

She watched him trying, and failing, to come to terms with it and said, "This is my life."

"It sucks," he said, and she surprised him by laughing.

"Yes."

"My mom is going to call me any minute, asking about it." He closed his eyes, thinking about it. "I could use a bag of Tootsie Rolls."

Nicole touched his arm. "No. I don't recommend going down that road."

He looked at her and whispered, "I'm *sorry*."

"I'm not. I had a really good time yesterday. At least before my father showed up."

"At least that didn't make it in the paper."

"It will, eventually. But I think it will be okay."

"*Was* it okay?"

She nodded. "I know them already. It's just strange now, suddenly having this connection. Having a father and a brother."

"A stepmother?"

She laughed. "Kind of. She's a real political wife, though. I'm sure she has some idea of how to leak this story to her benefit."

"Is that what you want?"

"What I want, I can't have. A mother and a father, together. Kids who were raised like. . . kids, I guess. I'd like to have known my brother when he was younger."

"I wish I hadn't known *my* brother when he was younger; he's better, a little, now. My sister was great growing up. But they still treat me like the baby of the family. They *never* let you forget."

Nicole said, "I know a little bit about no one letting you forget."

Flynn remembered, and knew he'd be forced to remember every time he saw the pictures. He deflated.

And now he knew why she always looked so unhappy. It was her mask, her costume.

But she was smiling at him right then so he just said, "Want to come to dinner tonight at my folks? You can meet the dream. My parents were high school sweethearts and they're still together, way too many years later."

Nicole paused, stepping away from him to put her already immaculate desk in order. Her eyebrows crinkled and she met his eyes.

"You just want me to tell your mom you didn't make me cry, don't you?"

Flynn threw his pride to the winds and begged. "*Please.*"

She laughed again.

She opened her mouth and then just stood there, thinking.

He said, "I know."

She focused on him and he waved his hands between them.

"I know that *this* is just some crazy. . . craziness. You've just, obviously, lost your mind from the stress of your runway and new store, and I'm taking advantage of that. I'm taking advantage of you."

Nicole tried not to laugh.

"And I'm not inviting you home with me to *meet* meet my parents. Because, first of all, my mom is crazy and she's way too old to be squeeing but she will. Be prepared for that. And my dad will be completely unimpressed with you. You might need to be prepared for that too, I don't know."

Nicole realized she was smiling stupidly at him. Hadn't even realized when her lips had migrated northward.

He bobbed on one foot. "But I just want to show you that it's not all that it's cracked up to be when your parents are still together. Because there's kissing and lap-sitting and comments that make you want to shoot bleach into your veins."

Nicole chuckled and Flynn shot her a look. "It's not cute, trust me."

"I do kind of want to see that."

"And I kind of want to show you it."

She nodded but said, "Flynn, you can't tell anyone about us. It won't end well."

He looked down at his suit. "No one would believe it anyway. I don't believe it."

"And your parents, don't tell them I'm coming. They'll tell someone. And someone will tell someone else and then they'll be cameras and a different kind of crazy craziness."

He stopped bouncing on one foot, and looked at her, and Nicole understood what he'd been saying about her and her looking because she had no clue what he was thinking.

He said, "Your world sucks, doesn't it?"

"Sometimes."

"I won't tell them even though it probably would go better if I warned them and you didn't see their initial reaction at meeting you."

Nicole stepped closer. "I think it's cute that you're trying to warn me about *your* mother. *Your* father."

He cocked his head. "Different kind of crazy is still crazy."

"Yes. We'll have to compare the crazy sometime, see which is worse." She smoothed his lapel with one hand thinking how he'd looked so sure of himself telling her he was taking advantage of her. "And I have to say it doesn't feel like I've lost my mind."

"You have. Trust me."

Nicole had been taken advantage of before, she could recognize it.

And she had good friends watching out for her who

would recognize it.

But Gia had high hopes for Flynn, and Victoria was unconcerned.

Maybe it was Nicole who was taking advantage of Flynn– and she knew suddenly that was right.

She was using him.

He was normal, when all Nicole had ever wanted was normal.

He was sweet, like Gia. Like during his formative years he'd only ever known good and would never really believe there was anything not good out there.

He was dependable and steady, here whenever she needed him. To fix whatever she needed fixing.

And she knew it wouldn't, couldn't, last.

She said, "What if it was me taking advantage of you?"

"I'd say, 'Oookkkaaaayyy,' like you'd lost your mind and I was just going along with you in case that meant you'd take advantage of me again."

She went to her tiptoes and his hands went to her waist. She said, "Oookkkaaaayyy."

And then when he didn't get it, whispered, "That was me just going along with you, hoping you'd take advantage of me again."

"See, I thought that was what you meant. And then I thought nah. And then you whispered to me and I stopped thinking."

Nicole kissed him, still smiling. Not caring at all that one of them must be taking advantage of the other.

Flynn stared at the ceiling, hiding behind Nicole's desk and missing the close walls of his closet.

"I can't believe I'm going to say this but my office is better for this."

She turned her head to smile at him and he said, "Less people need me than need you." He'd had a few heart-stopping minutes of wondering whether the locked door really was locked. "And, it's cozier."

She nodded. "Cloistered."

Flynn closed his eyes and held out his arms and operaed, "*Sanctuary!*"

She wouldn't sing it but she said, "Yes."

"We might be just a little bit messed up."

She laughed and said softly, "It's nice to be messed up with someone else for once."

"What about your sister?"

"We weren't together. It was me trying to protect her, and her trying to have fun. I don't know why I was afraid and she was excited."

Flynn reached for her hand. "Big sisters have to try and take care of their siblings. Little sisters, and brothers, have to try and have fun. It's the sibling code."

Nicole seemed to think about it. "Do you think so? That the reason she loved the chaos is because I didn't want her to?"

"Maybe."

"I don't understand her at all."

"It's probably mutual. That's the sibling code, too."

Nicole flipped to her side, propping her head on her hand, and Flynn tried to pay attention to the words coming out of her mouth and not her perfect naked body.

"You don't know my sister. She is everything ugly and horrifying and destructive about wealth and fame. One day, I'm going to get a call that she's OD'd and I can't do anything to stop it."

Flynn blinked a few times. "Wow. I don't even want to know what my sister thinks about me now."

Nicole's lips twitched. "She probably doesn't think that

about you. Unless you like to party harder than I know about."

"How old is your sister?"

"Seventeen."

Flynn sniffed and went back to looking at the ceiling. It was less distracting.

"My sister may have thought that about me when I was seventeen."

Nicole shook her head and lay back down next to him. "No. I bet when you were seventeen, your parties consisted of dwarves and elves and RPG all-nighters."

Tingle.

"Say dwarves and elves and RPG again."

Her shoulders shook with contained laughter and she said, "WOW. MMPG."

Tingle.

"Whose turn is it to take advantage? Yours?"

Nicole let the laughter out and rolled on top of him. "Thank you for making me laugh about my sister."

"You're welcome. And I really do think it will be okay. Big sisters are always going to think their siblings are hopeless at seventeen. You probably don't want to know what your seventeen-year-old sibling thinks of you."

"She thinks I'm a stick in the mud."

"Probably. I still think that about mine. But I love her."

Nicole stopped smiling and Flynn hurriedly changed the subject. "I'm really glad you decided to take advantage of me one last time before meeting my parents. You may feel free to completely ignore me tomorrow."

"It's not going to be that bad."

"Oh, it will be."

"I don't know. You're still standing after meeting Nikita. Maybe your parents will surprise you as well."

Flynn had blocked meeting Nikita from memory so he

just grunted as he stared into her eyes, tingling all over and telling himself he would be happy with whatever time he got with Nicole. Even if it ended tonight.

'Cause he was pretty sure it was going to.

Twenty-Six

Flynn pushed a hand through his hair and muttered, "This was a bad idea."

"It'll be okay."

"No. I don't know what I was thinking. Thank you for the ride out here, I'll take the train back."

He opened his door and Nicole said, "Flynn."

He sighed and hung his head. "Okay. Let's go in."

Flynn knocked loudly, then let himself in with his key and looked around the door. "Mom? Dad?"

"Oh, Flynn. Come in, what are you doing? Your dad's down on his computer, keeps asking if you're here yet. Mike! Flynn's here!"

"Um, I brought someone to dinner."

"Oh, good! Who is it, one of your friends? I'll just make some extra toast, there'll be plenty."

Flynn opened the door the rest of the way to let Nicole in and said, "Nicole Bissette, this is my mom, Lisa Redmond."

Lisa froze, a pile of laundry next to her on the living room couch and a half-folded undershirt on her lap.

She stared at Nicole. "Well, I. . ."

"It's nice to meet you, Mrs. Redmond. I hope you don't mind Flynn inviting me to dinner." She held out the bottle of red wine she'd brought despite Flynn telling her it was unnecessary.

Lisa stared at the bottle. "Oh, I. . ."

Flynn said, "Speechless is better than I was expecting."

Mike came up the basement stairs, saying, "I'm starving. I would have met you at the station," and Lisa jumped to her feet.

"Flynn! You should have told me we were going to have company!" Lisa looked at the load of laundry on the couch. "I was just folding– I'm just going to move– Come in, come in!" She grabbed an armful of clothes, then looked at the bottle in Nicole's hand still and lifted her chin.

"You can just put it right–"

"I'll take it, Mom."

"Okay. Wow, you're as pretty in person as you are in *People*. Nicole Bissette. I wish you'd told me, Flynn!"

"I told him not to, Mrs. Redmond. It's my fault."

"Oh, no! And please, you can call me Lisa. Or Mrs. Redmond! Whatever makes you comfortable." She laughed nervously. "Let me just go get rid of this."

They all watched as she ran down the hallway, socks and underwear falling unheeded.

Flynn cleared his throat. "And this is my dad, Mike. This is Nicole."

"The boss? Nice to meet you. Hungry?"

"Yes, thank–"

eeeeeeeeeeeeeeeeeeeeeeeeeeeeeeeeeeeeeeeeeeeeeeeeeeeeeee

Flynn looked up at the ceiling and away from the back bedrooms. "Told you."

Nicole squeezed his arm. "She went into another room. It doesn't count."

Mike narrowed his eyes at her hand on Flynn's arm, then clapped his hands together. "Well. Let's eat."

Lisa finally came out of the bedroom and served up toast and baked beans– actual homemade baked beans– and a generous helping of salad to a grateful Nicole.

And after a few stilted minutes, everyone forgot that she was famous.

Forgot that they didn't know her, and knew everything about her, all at the same time.

Lisa said, "Well, I know about *The Enquirer*. You can't believe everything you read," and Mike snorted.

Nicole wiped her mouth. "You can't believe any of it. Either the paper makes it up, or a celebrity's publicist makes it up."

Lisa said, "Not *People*?"

"Just stories. Official stories."

"My faith in the world is destroyed."

Nicole smiled with her eyes, and then she glanced at Flynn just sitting there knowing that whatever *this* was it was going to be over because his parents were wonderfully normal. She let the smile out at him, and then at Mike and Lisa.

Mike's fork hit his plate and his eyes widened. "Wow," he said and Lisa slapped his arm.

"I told you, she's gorgeous."

"You look just like–"

"Dad. Mom." Flynn glared at them, squinting one eye at them in the universal sign of *shut up*.

Nicole said, "It's okay."

And even if it wasn't okay, it was unchangeable.

Mike shook his head. "Sorry. I just didn't realize."

Lisa side-eyed him. "None of us wants to hear about

how you had a crush on *Nikita.*"

"It wasn't a crush. I just knew who she was, that's all."

Flynn put his hand on Nicole's arm and said sincerely, "Might I offer you a syringe full of bleach?"

Nicole laughed and Mike said, "Yeah, I'm just going to–"

He jerked his thumb over his shoulder and Flynn yelled, "Dad!"

"Go to the kitchen! Jeez!"

Mike pushed his chair back, muttering about a glass of water, and Lisa jumped up to follow him.

"Sorry. So sorry. Mike!"

Flynn blew out a breath. "Now they're going to whisper in the kitchen, thinking we can't hear."

Nicole put her chin in her hands, enjoying his embarrassment. Enjoying the whole normalness of the evening, of their family.

"It caught me off guard, Lisa."

"Go out there and apologize! To Flynn, too. You embarrassed him."

"Oh, I embarrassed him? I wasn't the one squealing like a teenage girl meeting one of The Monkees."

"The Monkees? Excuse me? Wait, you could hear me?! Why didn't you tell me!"

Flynn said loudly, "We can hear you now."

Silence greeted his announcement and Nicole giggled.

She said, "You were wrong."

Flynn shook his head in defeat. "I don't doubt it. What about?"

"It's cute."

"No!"

"They are."

"No!"

She reached for his hand under the table. "Thank you

for bringing me to meet your parents."

"Well, not *meet* meet, just like, you know, to study them."

"I know."

"And it's not over yet. You might still change your mind about the bleach."

Mike came out of the kitchen in time to see Nicole laugh and he stopped in his tracks. "Dammit," he said and whirled around and back into the kitchen.

"*Why didn't you warn me, Lisa?*"

"*That she looks like her mother? Pretty much it's a thing everybody knows.*"

"*I don't read* People!"

"*I know you don't. You just look at the pictures.*"

"*I do no–*"

"Still can hear you." Flynn sighed and said to no one in particular, "Could this night get any more embarrassing?"

Nicole squeezed his hand, still holding on to it under the table and still feeling very comfortable about it.

"You mean like if I saw that picture over there of you getting your Eagle Scout?"

He froze, his eyes round and his mouth puckered. He flicked his eyes to the wall.

"Dammit."

Nicole let go of his hand and stood to go take a better look at a teenaged Flynn.

"How old were you?"

"Sixteen. I blame peer pressure."

"It does account for a great deal of teenage misery. I like your glasses."

He joined her, looking at the dark thick rims and saying, "I blame peer pressure for those, too."

"I didn't know about the glasses. Contacts?"

"Surgery."

"Ah." She fingered the frame. "But I already knew you were a boy scout. The snacks in your desk, in case you get locked in."

He grimaced. "Be prepared. Can't hide it, can I?"

Nicole smiled. "No. I don't think we can hide who we are. Not for very long, at least."

Lisa and Mike came out of the kitchen, still whispering, and Flynn said, "Some of us don't even try."

"So cute."

She'd said it in all sincerity and Flynn just looked at her.

Then he turned and walked down the hallway and said, "Bleach, don't fail me now."

Twenty-Seven

Nicole was summoned home, and while she would have liked to send her mother a picture of a certain finger– or perhaps Nonna's evil eye– she went.

"I hear you had a lovely dinner with the Gearys."

"I did."

"I'm glad. I am! You don't have to look at me like that."

"I'm not looking at you any kind of way."

"Yes, you are. You're looking at me like I kept you from half your family for half your life and you're never going to forgive me."

Since Nicole *had* been thinking that, had been thinking that very thing since her lovely dinner with the Gearys, she just continued to look at her mother.

Who sighed theatrically and said, "Well, are you going to tell me about it?"

"No. It sounds like you already heard."

"Nicole, you are so very frustrating. Tell me what you thought about James. About Scott."

"About Cornelia?"

Nikita waved her hand. "I know enough about her."

That made Nicole's lips twitched and she said

grudgingly, "I thought James was comfortable. It was comfortable being around him."

"You do know him. I didn't keep you from him."

"Mm-hm. Little bit different now, but I was surprised to find it still was comfortable."

"Good, I'm glad. I am! Oh, for God's sake–"

Nicole laughed and Nikita paused and stared at her daughter. She sat up a little in her chair.

"And Scott?"

Nicole stopped laughing. Her mother may or may not have kept her father from her– in fair moments, Nicole could acknowledge that perhaps it hadn't been as isolated as she'd thought.

But Scott? Her brother?

She only knew him because they'd been in the same social circle, because he'd dated her best friend. She'd never spent any time with him, hadn't even had an inkling he could exist.

Nikita murmured, "I didn't realize that he would be so important to you."

"You didn't realize I would be upset at finding out I have a brother I know nothing about?"

"Half brother."

"Like Colette is my half sister?"

"It's different."

"It is, isn't it? Different because I got to grow up with her and I didn't get to grow up with him."

Nikita closed her eyes briefly. "Well."

"Different because he almost married my best friend and I had no idea. You couldn't have told me then?"

"I like to think I would have eventually," Nikita said and Nicole laughed humorlessly.

"Right."

"And then they broke up and there was no need. If I

may say, she overreacted a touch."

Nikita would think that. Maybe even Cornelia would think the same.

Nicole didn't.

"She overreacted to being cheated on? Or, to thinking she had been cheated on?"

Nicole still wasn't sure what she was supposed to think about it. Her loyalties were now divided and she couldn't seem to summon the outrage she'd once felt on her friend's behalf.

Nikita shifted in her seat. "You should ask him. He's family now, yes?"

"Oh, I hate you."

It came out cold and bitter and was answered the same way.

"Yes, but that is nothing new."

And it wasn't. Not new, so Nicole took a deep breath and blew it out as slowly and as silently as she could. She looked around the loft, knowing by the silence that Colette wasn't here. Even asleep, her sister had *presence*.

"Where is my other *half* sibling so early on a Sunday morning?"

"Out with friends."

At Nicole's silence, at the knowledge that Colette wasn't here on a Sunday morning only because she hadn't come home yet, her mother sighed again.

"Judge, judge, judge. It must be so exhausting to be you."

"Yes, incredibly exhausting to care. Incredibly exhausting to want to stop my seventeen-year-old sister from making mistakes that will change her life forever."

"Speaking of mistakes, how is your little office romance going?"

"Don't change the subject."

"There's nothing more to say about it because I won't *try* to control the future. And I can't change the past. And you won't forgive me. So let's talk about. . . what's his name?"

"No, thanks. And it's not a mistake."

"It is, just not yours. I assume he's the one who's mellowed you out enough to come visit? To laugh, even, and have a nice visit before we irritated each other into our usual bickering state." Nikita picked up the mirror on the side table next to her and inspected her now half-healed face. "He must be good in bed. . .good in closet. . .he must know what he's doing."

Nicole stood up and her mother said softly to her mirror, "Be kind to him. It can't last, and it never ends well for a man in love with a Bissette."

"You would know."

"Yes, I would."

"And he's not. In love with me."

Nikita looked around the mirror, laughing, and then said, "Oh, you're serious. Nicole, really. Don't be stupid. Of course he's in love with you."

"No, he's not. We both know this is just. . ."

Just some crazy craziness.

"Just a fling."

Nikita said, "If I was the type of controlling mother you imagine you'd want, I would have something to say here."

"Oh, finally I can be happy you aren't."

Nikita went back to her mirror. "Have your fling, darling. Please, let me know how it ends. It's an indulgence, I know, but I always enjoy a good soap opera."

Twenty-Eight

Flynn had his legs up on his desk again. Watching *Captain America: The First Avenger* this time because hey, he had to break it up sometimes. A guy couldn't only watch *The IT Crowd*.

But he'd seen it before and it was late and his mind was wandering.

Thinking about the website.

He'd pushed and worked so hard and now it was up and running and checking on it was now part of the routine.

So strange how that could happen.

New and exciting becomes normal and ho-hum.

Then he was thinking about his family.

His mom kept calling him and leaving messages about how great Nicole was.

Flynn didn't disagree, but it did reaffirm that taking her home to not meet the parents was a mistake.

His brother had called, which had surprised Flynn so much that he'd actually answered the phone instead of letting it go to voicemail.

"Mom thinks you're dating Nicole Bissette."

"Yeah, that was a mistake."

". . .are you dating Nicole Bissette?"

"No."

He was *sleeping* with Nicole Bissette. There was a difference, big one, and probably his brother and his mother would keel over from shock if they found out.

His brother said, "Good. For a second there, I thought I might have to go back to church in case it was the end of the world."

Might be fun to watch his brother keel over but Flynn said, "Har. Har."

"Dad needs help with the computer again. Call him, will ya. I don't have time."

"I was *just* there. He didn't mention it."

"'Course not. He was looking at your boss's rack."

Flynn said, "Great talking to you, bro," and hung up on his brother's laughter.

Should have let it go to voicemail, because next time Flynn saw his brother, he was going to have to knock his block off.

And now he was thinking about Nicole.

About how he sure was glad he wasn't dating Nicole.

Was glad he didn't have to get all ruffled when his brother was inappropriate about her.

Was glad he didn't have to think too hard about his dad having a crush on her mother. . .

Yeah, didn't need to think about that ever again, no matter what.

Was glad he didn't have to tell his mother that he was dating Nicole Bissette.

Glad, he said.

He stood up, rolling his shoulders and turning off Steve Rogers.

Flynn knew he shouldn't have taken Nicole home. Knew that was all his family was ever going to talk about.

Working for Nicole Bissette was all they talked about when he first started but after he hardly ever even talked to her, it had died down.

Now he was talking to her, bringing her to dinner. . .

His mom had already told him to invite her over again– one of the seven messages she'd left for him since that night– and maybe if they *were* dating, he would have.

Maybe.

He'd have to sit his dad down and give him some ground rules.

His mom, too.

But they weren't dating.

No, it was just some crazy craziness.

And it was.

Crazy. Craziness.

And, please, let him do the crazy craziness with her again.

But it was sad, too. Because it was almost normal.

Because like building a website overnight, it was exhilarating and new and exciting.

And then it was normal.

And then, you wanted more.

Flynn blew out his breath, deciding he needed to go home.

It was late and everyone had left already, even Nicole. She'd had somewhere to be and someone to meet and because they weren't dating, he couldn't ask.

Hell, maybe she was *on* a date. Maybe she'd had to leave early to get ready. Put on a slinky black dress that wouldn't gape and red lipstick that wouldn't smear.

Maybe she was out having dinner.

Not smiling at someone else.

And then suddenly *yes* smiling. Suddenly *laughing* at someone else.

Making someone else's heart knock against his chest like it was trying to kill him in this perfect moment so that it could never become normal.

Flynn grabbed the doorknob tightly and twisted.

And twisted again.

"You have got to be kidding me," he said to the empty- locked- room.

Twenty-Nine

Nikita's voice had echoed over and over in Nicole's head until she'd picked up the phone and called her father.

You should ask him. He's family now, yes?

Had asked James for her brother's phone number and listened as his voice filled with pleasure, and Scott had answered his phone and agreed to meet her for dinner, sounding like he might enjoy the experience.

He'd ordered drinks for them right away and said, "I don't know how this is going to go between us when Father is not here to insult."

Nicole didn't think there was any way this dinner would turn out well since she was going to ask him if he cheated on her best friend.

If she could actually work up the nerve to do it.

She said, "Do you really think there could be more? Of us?"

More siblings. And Nicole honestly didn't know if it would be good or bad.

Sad, but maybe not bad.

Scott said, "I don't know but I don't like the odds. You'd think he could have bothered to mention you at some point in the last twenty or so years."

"Twenty-seven. And you'd think. But maybe he just didn't know how to bring it up," she said, not knowing how to bring up her own awkward subject.

Scott eyed her as he ordered, and when the waiter left, said, "I'm twenty-nine. At least there are a few years between us. And you sound like you're just going to forgive him."

"No. Yes." She looked down into her glass, then sipped. "My mother, I won't forgive. But James. . . I don't know him well enough to really hate."

"It's okay, sis. I'll hate him for you."

Nicole nodded her head. "Thank you," she said and Scott laughed.

He said, "And maybe you wouldn't hate him anyway. My mother knew and didn't tell me. I don't hate her. Maybe it's some messed up mother-son, father-daughter bull. Maybe I think it wasn't her place to tell even though my father would have done it if she'd told him to. Maybe you think James couldn't, that *your* mother wouldn't let him, when we both know he still could have, if he wanted to."

Nicole stared at him, and he shrugged and took another drink.

"It's just a theory."

"It is kind of strange though, isn't it? That I hold my mother fully responsible."

"And I hold my father fully responsible."

It could have been, though, that not telling her was just one more thing with her mother, and the first thing with her father.

Small salads were placed in front of them and they both sat there, lost in their own thoughts until Scott said, "Well, it doesn't matter. He should have told me." He looked up.

"And there, I've forgiven myself for not forgiving him. I feel better already."

Nicole smiled at him, and Scott cocked his head.

"When I was almost engaged to your best friend, I never saw you smile."

"No, I don't with most people."

He studied her face. "I can see why. But, you're smiling at me now."

"You're my brother now. And I want you to feel comfortable enough so I can ask you something really uncomfortable."

"Well, at least you're honest about it."

"It's about my best friend."

Scott made a face into his glass. "Sorry I brought her up."

She just looked at him, not wanting to ruin the evening so early, but he swallowed his drink and sighed.

"Go ahead."

"Did you?"

Scott took a deep breath. "No."

Nicole said, "I'm sorry."

Sorry that she believed him. Sorry that they'd both had to go through that when there'd been no reason.

Sorry that she felt like she had to tell Victoria.

Scott said, "Sometimes I am, too. And then I remember that she obliterated me from her life for some stupid story. She never even gave me a chance." He shrugged one shoulder. "If it was going to happen, I'm glad it happened then and not later. Like our golden anniversary."

"Can I tell her?" she asked and he speared a tomato with force.

"It doesn't matter."

"It does."

"It won't change anything, and I don't want you or her

thinking it will. That bridge disintegrated in a fiery ball of napalm."

"Scott." She waited for him to look up and then said, "She should know. What she threw away."

"I thought you were on her side."

"She's my best friend. That doesn't mean I don't know what she's like. That doesn't mean she shouldn't be told she's wrong every once in a while."

"You willing to throw away your friendship on it?"

Nicole wouldn't be throwing away her friendship. Might be bringing down a little friendly fire on herself.

Family, both the blood kind and the heart kind, sometimes required sacrifices.

Scott shook his head. "Nicole. Don't do it. It's not worth it."

"I'm not doing it for you because you're right. It's not going to change anything. But her father–"

"Is a piece of work?"

Victoria's father was just like her, only worse.

Nicole said, "She knows what he is. But sometimes she forgets. Sometimes she thinks she wants to be like him."

"I get it, you know. He didn't think I was good enough for his precious daughter. When push came to shove, she didn't either."

"Does it help any to think that maybe it's one of those messed up father-daughter bull things? That he essentially told her to choose between you or him, and she chose him?"

"I don't know if that helps. And I wouldn't want someone I loved to have to choose between me or her father." He put down his fork, pushed away his plate. "I sure do want someone who would, though."

She nodded because that actually sounded quite lovely.

"Nicole, I don't want to know what Victoria says, okay?

If she believes you when she never believed me, I will jump into the Hudson. And it probably won't kill me, just ruin a good suit and make my hair smell for days. Let's just not even go there."

She sighed. "Okay."

"Okay. . . You could maybe tell me if she cries a little."

Nicole raised her eyebrows.

"Or if she disowns her father."

Nicole shook her head.

"If she feels really, really bad."

Nicole chuckled quietly. "I know she will."

"Maybe you should leave me out of it completely. If she obliterates you from her life for telling her, I'll have to go find her and beat her up. I've never been a big brother before but that seems to figure prominently in the job description."

Nicole blinked. "Uh. It won't come to that but. . . thank you?"

He nodded. "You're welcome. What else are big brothers supposed to do?" He snapped his fingers. "You got any boyfriends you need vetted?"

"No."

She thought of Flynn, then, and his sibling code. How older siblings were supposed to worry about their younger siblings. And younger siblings were supposed to have fun so they could make their older siblings worry.

"There's someone. Not a boyfriend."

"Who is it?"

"No one you know."

"Right. If we have any kind of luck, it'll be *my* best friend."

She smiled at him. "It's not. It's someone I work with."

He blinked, thinking about it. "Your boss?"

"Um, I own my own company?"

"So when it all goes south, you can just fire him? There's nothing for me to do in this scenario."

"Sorry. I only recently found out about you."

"Next time you start something, take into account that you have an older brother now, will you?"

You have an older brother now.

And it felt good.

She grabbed her drink, blinking quickly to push back sudden, happy, tears.

She cleared her throat. "Yes. This will take some getting used to. Having an older brother to fix all my problems for me."

He grinned at her.

"You know, Nicole, I'm glad that when I discovered I had a sister, I didn't hate her."

"Me, too."

He chuckled. "You *did* hate me. You were obligated to."

"You're right, I was and I did. And maybe it's one of those brother-sister bull things, but it died fairly quickly. I'm glad that when I found out I had a brother, it turned out to be you."

He said, "Me, too."

They smiled at each other, Nicole thinking that all the trouble of family was sometimes worth it.

Scott finally said, "We should enjoy this while it lasts because the new car smell will probably wear off."

"Probably."

"Probably right when I start wondering if having a sister is going to affect my inheritance at all."

Nicole choked on the drink she'd just taken. She patted her lips until she stopped coughing and then grinned at her brother.

"I would be surprised if it did considering James set up a trust for me at birth."

"Hmm. Maybe." He froze. "Wait a minute, do you have access to it already?"

"Yes."

Scott made a tight fist and muttered through clenched teeth, "Damn him, that is completely unfair." He looked at her and said with relish, "And I will *never* forgive him."

After dinner, they both checked their messages and Nicole smiled when she saw she had one from Flynn.

SOS. Locked in closet.

She chuckled, imagining him in there with his snacks and his movies, and then saw Scott looking at her.

He nodded at her phone. "This the not-boyfriend?"

She couldn't get the smile off her face, so just nodded happily as she texted back.

Just need to find a phone booth and then I'll fly right over.

She stood and Scott helped her into her coat. "Booty call calls. You sure you don't need me to be your muscle, make him show you a little respect?"

She patted his arm absently as she got another message. "I'm sure. But I'll keep that in mind for next time because you sound like you'd really enjoy it."

It's a bird! A plane! My boss! Wait a minute. . .

Scott shrugged into his own coat. "You know, I think I really would. As long as he's not a hulking brute." He tried to get a peek of her phone. "You're not into hulking brutes, are you?"

She held it away from him. "I haven't been yet. But like I said, maybe next time."

He coughed out a laugh. "We're getting the hang of this, aren't we?"

"I think so. I'm just going to let him know I'll be there as soon as I can get rid of you."

She grinned while she typed, *ETA twenty minutes*, and when she looked back up Scott was typing on his own phone.

"Hang on, just letting our father know about your big hulking brute of a boyfriend. Maybe he can get a background check done on him. Or maybe pay him a little visit to scare him off. I'm sure neither one of us would approve of him."

Nicole grabbed for his phone, laughing when she saw he wasn't texting at all but playing a game.

"My not-boyfriend has been warned off by both my mother and Victoria. What's James going to do to scare him?"

Scott sucked in a breath. "Nikita and Victoria, and he's still booty calling you? Okay, I kind of want to meet this guy."

Nicole stopped, thought about it. She didn't know if she wanted her new brother not-meeting her not-boyfriend.

She said, "Seems like it would be awkward."

"Well, yeah, *tonight* would be awkward. Don't want to bring your brother to your booty call."

"It's not a booty call. He's locked in a closet." She found Flynn's first message and held it up for Scott to see.

He stared at it, stuffing his hands in his pocket. "Is that. . .some sort of. . .code?"

"No, it's not some kind of code. He's locked in a closet."

"And it's nothing sexual?"

"Nope."

"Maybe I don't need to meet him."

Nicole smiled, then quickly kissed Scott on the cheek. "Thanks for meeting me for dinner. I'd like to do it again."

"Me, too. Sis. I'll give you a call."

Thirty

Nicole knocked lightly on Flynn's closet door, then put her key in and turned. She pushed the door in lightly and there he was with his feet up on his desk and his hand in a bag of Doritos.

She said, "Hey."

"Hey."

He looked at her briefly, then away. Embarrassed, maybe.

"I see your snacks came in handy."

"Maybe we should take the lock off the outside of the door."

She laughed, coming inside to sit on the edge of his desk. "It's probably a good idea. What are you watching?"

"*Superman*. I was seeing if he ever got locked in a closet."

"Did he?"

"No." He cleared his throat. "I'm sorry I ruined your date."

She cocked her head. "Are you?"

"No."

"Oh, good. Because it wasn't a date. I was having

dinner with my brother."

Flynn let out a breath. "Oh. Good." He sat up, taking his feet off the desk. "I mean, I'm still sorry I ruined your evening. Just glad it wasn't a date. That I was ruining."

"You didn't ruin anything. I'm glad that you texted me and didn't stay in here all night long."

"That was my first idea, but then I drank one of my Red Bulls."

"Ah. Not as prepared as you thought you were?"

"I did not take into account the fact that what goes in must come out."

"Do you need to. . ." She pointed out the door and he shook his head convincingly.

Then he nodded. "Yes, rather desperately."

She laughed. "Then go!"

He jumped up, dashing out of the closet and down the hall, and Nicole just let herself laugh.

She sat down in his chair and pushed play, watched *Superman* on screen while she waited for her Clark Kent to come back.

When he saw her sitting in his chair, he leaned against the door jamb, and she said, "What are doing now that you don't have to spend the night in here?"

"Probably go finish watching *Superman* at home."

"Oh."

"Why?"

She shrugged. "I was kind of hoping you'd take advantage of me again."

Flynn blinked. He pushed himself to his feet and came inside the room. He closed his laptop with one finger.

She stayed sitting, looking up at him.

He said slowly, "I don't want you thinking I don't want to take advantage, it's just going to take me a second to switch gears. I spent the evening thinking you were on a date."

"There's no one I'm not-dating, except you."

He looked up at the ceiling, repeating what she'd said silently, his finger moving with the words.

She slipped her hand into his and he looked down at her.

"I had a really nice dinner with my brother. And then you texted me and I wanted to tell you about it."

His hand curled around hers and the distant look in his eyes went away.

He confessed, "I didn't lock myself in here on purpose. But I wasn't not unhappy that it would cut your evening short."

She looked at the ceiling, mouthing his words, then said, "This is getting confusing."

"Getting? I thought we arrived at confusing a few weeks ago."

She looked in his eyes, then down at their hands. "My brother wants to not-meet you but maybe he could just meet you instead. We could unconfuse one thing at least."

Flynn didn't say anything and Nicole kept looking at their hands.

He cleared his throat. "Meet me or *meet* meet me?"

She looked up again, a thousand voices in her head.

Okay, just two.

One that was happily declaring, *I have very high hopes for Flynn.*

And one predicting gloomily that *It never ends well for a man in love with a Bissette.*

Nicole met his eyes and whispered, "*Meet* meet you."

"Really?"

She nodded. "But you know how you warned me that meeting your parents wasn't a good idea?"

"Yes. I haven't forgotten that I was right."

"This is another one of those things that isn't a good idea."

"Maybe it will be okay. Maybe I'll think it's *cute*."

She wanted to smile at him, wanted to believe he could think her life was, if not cute, then at least bearable.

She told the truth instead.

"It won't be and it's not. I still want to do it."

He froze. "Let me be very clear here. The thing that isn't a good idea, that you still want to do, is date me. Right?"

"Yes."

And Nicole suddenly realized this feeling was happiness.

Whenever she was with Flynn, she was happy. Light, like suddenly life wasn't weighing her down anymore. Light, like the sun was shining brightly after a particularly long winter.

He was her sugar. He made everything better, no nasty side effects.

He was silly and true and uncomplicated.

A boy scout.

She smiled and said again, "Yes."

He leaned down, stopping when his lips were a breath away from hers.

He whispered, "I would love to meet your brother. I would love to date you."

"It's not going to be easy."

"Okay."

"*I'm* not easy."

He smiled. "Okay."

She put her lips on his. Kissed him while she looked into his eyes.

Heard one more voice in her head before she heard nothing at all.

Don't be stupid, Nicole. Of course he's in love with you.

Thirty-One

Flynn took her back to his apartment and they watched the rest of *Superman* cuddled in his bed.

Naked.

He was pretty sure he was dreaming and he'd wake in the morning to find he was hunched over his desk, his face stuck to the keyboard, and still locked in his closet.

But when he awoke, he was in his bed. Nicole still next to him.

Still naked.

She opened her eyes and said, "Hey."

"Hey."

And that was all he had, so he just looked at her. Probably smiling at her like a goof because her eyes were crinkling at him.

Smeyesing.

He'd been working with models too long if he knew that term.

But he thought it with a happy sigh and a *damn wasn't he the luckiest man alive* grin.

She sighed, too. But it wasn't a happy one. It was worried.

Flynn said, "We don't have to tell anyone."

Nicole rolled away from him and stared up at the ceiling.

She shook her head. "I've warned you, and I think that is all I can do about it. And I've decided that I'm not going to worry. I was so worried about the store. And then we did it. And it was nothing. Worrying is overrated."

Flynn nodded. "Yes. I decide, too. No worrying. Not that I was worrying before but I like how it sounds. *I decide.*"

Nicole flicked her eyes at him. "Are you making fun of me?"

"No! Am I? I don't think I am. I just like how that sounds. *I decide.*"

His phone rang and Flynn lunged to the nightstand with a muttered *thank God* that turned into an *oh, God* when he checked who was calling.

He answered with a loud and boisterous, "Hi, Mom!" that made Nicole smile.

Don't shout into the phone, Flynn. I like my hearing just the way it is.

He pointed at the phone and mouthed to Nicole, "My mom!"

Nicole said, in a normal tone of voice, "Tell her hello from me."

Who was that? A girl?

"It's my boss. Because I'm at work. Early start today."

Nicole? Say hello from me. Say it.

"My mom says hi."

Nicole leaned forward. "Hello, Lisa."

Oh, Nicole! Hello! Is my son working hard for you?

One corner of Nicole's lips turned up. "He always does."

Oh, that's good. You two should come to dinner again, tell us how the website is doing. Tell Flynn to bring you to dinner on Saturday.

"I'm right here, Mom. I put you on speakerphone."

Take me off speaker, take me off speaker!

"Why? You were talking to both of us."

Because I sound funny on speaker. Take me off speaker right this instant, Flynn.

"Okay, I'm going to go. We'll see you Saturday for dinner."

Wait. She said yes?

"She just nodded yes at me. And she's doing it again. That's a yes for dinner. We are go for dinner."

Oh no, what am I going to wear?

"Bye, Mom."

Flynn put his phone back and stared at Nicole. "Was that you not worrying about my mom blabbing to her neighbor or her dentist or the grocery store bagger that you're going to be at her house for dinner on Saturday?"

She nodded. Took a deep breath.

"Yes."

"And how's that working for you?"

"Pretty sure it was a mistake."

"I'm going to call my mom back. Tell her not to tell anyone."

Nicole nodded. Took a deep breath.

And said, "Okay."

Thirty-Two

After Nicole's brush with not worrying, and realizing that was never ever going to go well for her, she texted Victoria before she could change her mind.

Call me when you get a minute.

She didn't expect an answer right away so she was surprised to hear her phone ding with Victoria's reply.

That'll be next year. Important?

Kind of. It can wait.

Do I need to peel the skin off F?

Nicole tried to slow her suddenly racing heartbeat. *No! He's great.*

I'll try to get a minute at lunch.

Nicole wrote, *OK. Anytime,* so she shouldn't have been surprised that she was in the bathroom when her friend called her.

She didn't dare not answer.

"I was sure you would call tomorrow. Maybe next week."

Victoria's tired voice sounded dejected. "I needed a break. It's been a rough week."

"I'm sorry. The moron's footwear troubling you even

more than usual?"

Victoria chuckled softly. "I want to say that he improved unexpectedly. But then he turned up in flip-flops with white athletic socks."

"No, he didn't!"

"Oh, yes he did. He looked like he had, I don't know, two really weird toes. Like a camel hoof."

Nicole snickered. "Are you saying that he had camel toes?"

Victoria barked a laugh. "Well, that's a new definition but that's what it looked like. I think to myself everyday that he can't possibly get any worse. And then he does."

"No wonder you needed a break. The horror!"

Nicole could hear the smile in her friend's voice. "You can't imagine. And while I would like to lay all my problems at Jace's feet, Dad's not doing well out here either."

Nicole pushed her fist into her belly and whispered, "I'm sorry, Victoria."

"I thought it would be okay. I thought if we had the nurse pretend she was his secretary and that we made him an office out here, that it would be familiar enough. He's been to San Francisco plenty of times."

Nicole had never spent a lot of time with Victoria's father but had heard how at first he couldn't remember where he was going, or how to get somewhere he'd been a hundred times before.

How he couldn't remember where he'd put something down yesterday but things that had happened twenty years ago were fresh and new. And he relived it over and over. Talked about it over and over. Stuck in his own personal hell.

Victoria said, "He's so confused and he can't remember. He thinks I'm my mother."

"I hope your mother during the good years."

"Would that be better? I wonder. But no."

"I'm so sorry. Is there anything I can do to help?"

"No. But it's nice to talk to you." Victoria sighed. "It's nice to talk to a woman. Men, men, men as far as the eye can see."

"And you're complaining?"

"About these men? Yes." Victoria chuckled evilly. "Although they do have good taste in music. But let's not give any more stupid men any more of our limited time. What did you need to talk about?"

Nicole chewed on her lip. "It's just more stupid men. We can talk about it later."

Victoria sighed out a long, tired breath.

"Let's do it now. Who knows when I can get away from the zoo again."

"It's about your dad."

"My dad? What could you possibly–" Victoria words cutoff and her breath sped up and she said harshly, "Scott."

"We can talk about it later."

Silence. Nothing.

"Victoria?"

Still more nothing, until Victoria said very quietly, "Are you on my side?"

"I love you, and I will always have your back."

She did, and she would. Victoria and Gia had been her sisters for too long for that to ever go away.

Victoria said, "Except now you have a brother."

"I asked him."

More silence, so Nicole whispered, "He said he didn't cheat on you. I believe him."

"Maybe now's not a good time to talk about this."

"Okay. I'm sorry."

"I gotta go. Can only deal with ten problems at a time,

an eleventh will just put me over the edge."

Nicole said, "Okay, call me when you can," but Victoria had already hung up, leaving Nicole sitting on her porcelain throne.

Cold, inside and out.

Thirty-Three

Flynn made sure Nicole wasn't coming over that evening before heading out to his parent's house.

This talk needed some eye contact.

Some sit down and listen to these rules before I have to call upon the hammer of Thor to knock some sense into you.

Harder to do with his parents than he was expecting, mainly because the minute he walked in the door his mom was alternating fussing over him and berating him for not bringing Nicole.

"Mom. Stop. Where's Dad?"

"Where do you think?"

"Dad! Can you come up here?"

Mike trooped up the stairs. "You missed dinner."

"It's okay. I came to talk to you and mom."

They exchanged a *look* and Lisa said innocently, "About what?"

"I think you know about what. Sit down."

Mike's eyebrows rose at the tone, but they both sat down on the couch.

Flynn put his hands behind his back and paced in front

of them, looking down at the carpet and trying to get his thoughts in order.

Lisa nudged Mike with her shoulder and wiggled her eyebrows.

Mike said, "Son–"

"Okay, this is how it's going to go." Flynn stopped pacing and turned toward them. "I am dating Nicole."

Lisa jumped to her feet. "I knew it!" She turned to Mike. "I told you it was too early for him to be at work."

"I like her, okay? And for some reason–" Flynn shook his head because he just couldn't believe it "–she likes you guys. She agreed to come to dinner again after the last fiasco. *And there will be no more fiascos.*"

Mike said, "That seems unlikely but okay."

"I mean it. No going to the kitchen to be alone with thoughts about her mother. Gross. No more talk of *People*, and squealing, for God's sake. No squealing."

"You should have warned me."

"You're right. That's why I'm warning you now."

Lisa made a face. "I can try. What if she just casually mentions someone famous?"

"Then you will casually not squeal."

Mike looked at his wife doubtfully. "You ask a lot from your mom, kid. What are we getting in return?"

"What are you–" Flynn closed his open mouth with a snap. "How about I keep coming home for dinner? How about I keep fixing your computer for you? How about I get to keep my insanely beautiful girlfriend! How about you get to stop asking if I've met a girl yet!"

Mike said, "He makes some good points."

Lisa nodded her head at her husband. "He does, and I'm willing to try. I just need. . ."

"A game plan?"

"Yes!" She held her hands up to Flynn. "I understand

the no squealing, I do. But what am I supposed to do instead? Can *I* go to the kitchen?"

"And stick your head in the oven?"

Mike half stood. "Hey! Don't talk to your mother like that."

Flynn shoved his hands in his hair, turning to stare at the TV.

"Sorry. I'm sorry. You guys are stressing me out. This is never going to work."

Lisa pushed her husband back down, joining him on the couch.

"It's okay. He didn't mean it," she said quietly and Mike said, "I don't care if he didn't mean it. I'm going to knock his block off if he does it again."

Flynn spun back around. "I know, you can go to the bathroom. Flush the toilet and run the water and squeal into a towel."

Mike thought about it, then nodded. "That might work."

Lisa said, "Okay, I can do that. What about your dad?"

Mike shifted in his seat. "Nah. I don't need a game plan."

Lisa said, "Oh, yeah. Right," and Flynn said, "You were *real* smooth."

"What? It was Nikita sitting at my dining room table, it took me by surprise is all, and it's not going to happen again."

Flynn asked, dead-eyed, "It's not?"

"One and done."

"Because her name is what now?"

"Nicole, I know. She just looks like Nikita. When she smiles. And sounds like her when she laughs."

Lisa rolled her eyes. "I'll give him a safety pin. He can keep it in his pocket and jab himself in the leg when the resemblance is too much to bear."

Mike said, "I'm not going to– Yeah, okay, that's a good idea."

Flynn nodded between them. "Okay. Okay. We got a game plan." He held out his hand. "Seal the deal, Mom."

His mother looked at his hand, then chuckled as she shook it. "I will try my best not to embarrass you in front of your girlfriend. Who happens to be Nicole Bissette. Squee!" She laughed. "It doesn't count if I say it and not do it, right? And, if I squee when Nicole is not around, do I make a sound?"

"Yes." Flynn held his hand out to his dad. "This is going to be a disaster."

Mike grabbed and shook, squeezing Flynn's hand hard enough to make him squint with pain.

"You've given it your best, son. But yes, it will be a disaster."

"Thanks, Dad."

Mike let go of his hand. "Just doing my best to prepare you."

"Yeah. I'm prepared for disaster, I don't need any help with that department. And hey, will you talk to Barrett? Because if he talks about Nicole's rack again, I will have to kill him."

Lisa gasped. "He said *what*? Any son of mine talking disrespectfully about a woman. . ."

She jumped to her feet, racing for the phone, and Mike said, "It's all right. Your mother will kill him for you."

Mike took a deep breath and leaned back against the couch.

"Is she really worth all this trouble, son?"

"Yeah, Dad. She's worth any trouble."

Mike made a face. "Just because she's beautiful and famous?"

"Because she makes me feel like I'm Superman. Even when I'm locked in a closet waiting for her to rescue me, I feel like I can save the world."

Mike blinked slowly. "Do I want to know about the closet?"

Flynn shook his head. "No."

His dad frowned. He nodded his head.

And then he pushed himself from the couch and patted his son on the shoulder.

"Well, then. See you guys on Saturday. Don't be late for dinner."

Thirty-Four

Nicole was tucked in Flynn's bed Friday night and not paying much attention to the movie, although he was enjoying watching Thor.

I mean, Thor was fun to look at. And, Nicole had to admit, there was Loki.

Loki was always distracting when he was on screen.

But there was lots of room left in her brain for worrying.

About Victoria. All alone out in San Francisco with her dad.

Taking on too much and sounding like she was drowning in it.

And Nicole heaping more on her at the worst possible time.

She should have waited. Should have left it alone.

She'd called Gia and told her to hound Victoria. Make sure she was okay. And that was all she could do right now about her best friend.

There was also dinner tomorrow with the parents.

Flynn was worried about it, which was making her worry about it.

Not so much about the parents because she'd already met them.

But now that they were dating... Well, there was more to worry about.

Someone would get hold of the information soon. And then they'd start hounding every part of his life trying to find out who he was, where he came from.

And then his adorable parents would start getting hounded and then they wouldn't be happy to see her anymore.

Nicole looked down at Flynn's hand holding hers. Short, clean nails but not perfect and not polished.

He wasn't polished.

And she could see the headlines already, tearing him apart.

And then he wouldn't be smiling at her over a movie either.

But she wouldn't look at the headlines and she wouldn't read the comments.

She *wouldn't*.

And she wouldn't let him either.

She *couldn't*.

Nicole was incredibly grateful for the distraction from worrying when her phone rang and it was Scott.

"Hey, sis. Quick question. On a scale of one to ten, how horrifying is it that your sister came on to me?"

Nicole sat up as she heard Colette's voice, faint but snotty.

Oh, you so wish.

Scott ignored her to say, "I mean, I get that we're not really related. No blood at least. But isn't it: The sister of my sister is my sister?"

The sister of your sister is your enemy. *I am now!*

Nicole said, "It's still pretty horrifying."

Scott sighed. "Another quick question. How old is she?"

"She's seventeen."

Nicole could hear Colette rolling her eyes.

Why is everyone so hung up on that?

Scott pulled the phone away from his mouth to say to Colette, "It's a thing and it's called *underage*. You'll understand when you're older. Or when some guy goes to jail because you told him you were nineteen."

He put the phone back up to say to Nicole, "Well, then, I think I found something that belongs to you and could you come get her?"

I don't belong to her.

Scott said, "Jail bait. Hoo-haa-haa."

Oh, I can totally tell you're related to Nicole.

Nicole said, "How bad is it?"

"She's flying. I've crashed and burned."

Nicole sighed. "I'll be right there."

She found them in the back of the club, side by side on a red velvet couch, both of their arms folded and both of them glaring at the other, unspeaking.

Relief crossed Scott's face when he saw her. Colette rolled her eyes and looked away.

Scott jumped to his feet. "I'm sorry I had to call you but she was all over me and then she was Colette Bissette and then I needed a shower, stat. This is what I was talking about! We could be related to anybody here and we wouldn't know it!"

Colette deigned to look at her sister. "There is seriously something wrong with that side of your family. I always thought it was just you. But anytime anyone comes over to see if I'm okay, and I'm *not*, he says in this deep voice like he's manly, 'She's seventeen, bro. Save your rescue for someone who can thank you for it.' So not funny."

"So not," Scott mimicked. "So thank you for coming so quickly."

He jerked his chin at Flynn standing quietly behind Nicole. "Who's this?"

Flynn reached around, holding his hand out. "Flynn. Hi."

Scott shook it reflexively, then looked at his watch. "Kind of late for a date, isn't it? This the not-boyfriend?"

Nicole took Flynn's hand. "Just boyfriend, now."

Colette stood, running her eyes up and down Flynn. "Oh, Nikita was not lying. You're dating? Him?"

Scott folded his arms at Flynn. "Upgraded, huh?"

Colette smirked at her sister. "Now you're going to see how *annoying* he can be."

Scott glanced down at her, then unfolded his arms. "Nope, I'm done for tonight because I still need to go wash my sister's sister off me."

Colette made a face. "You're disgusting."

"You're family. It is disgusting."

"You *wish* you were my family."

"Why would I wish that you little–"

Nicole stepped between them. "Okay. Thank you, Scott, for finding my sister. I'll get her home."

"Better you than me. She's going to scream bloody murder when she gets close enough to the bouncer."

Colette sucked in a breath, then bit down hard, her jaw jutting out with force, and Scott was the one smirking this time.

"Called it, didn't I? Why do you think we're hiding in this corner?"

"Because you're a perv? That was my guess."

Scott gave Nicole a truly disgusted look. "I made out with my sister's seventeen-year-old sister so I can't really argue with her, can I?"

Nicole was afraid her face was agreeing with him but she tried anyway.

"It'll be okay. Tomorrow. She probably won't even remember."

"I can only hope. Maybe I'll go find something to make myself forget. After my shower."

He nodded at Flynn, heading for the stairs and outside.

Colette called after him, "Bye, Scotty! Call me!"

He jerked to a stop, then turned on his heel and headed for the bar instead.

Nicole blew out a breath and jerked her thumb over her shoulder. "Let's go."

Colette folded her arms. "No."

Nicole debated if they were ever going to get her sister out the door without her cooperation and then pulled out her phone.

She dialed.

She put the phone to her ear.

Colette asked, "Who are you calling?"

"The police."

Colette blinked. "What?"

"My seventeen-year-old sister has been accosted in this club. And she's high. I think she's been roofied."

"Are you crazy? I've got my fake ID and I was accosted by your brother!"

"Did you. . ."

"Give him the best night he's ever likely to get? No! He flipped out when I told him my name!"

"Oh, good. I'd hate for him to be charged with statutory rape. That can ruin a man's life. And I guess when they test your blood, it's not going to be Rohypnol, either," Nicole said, and then into the phone, "I can hold."

"Okay, stop. Just hang up. Tell them it was a mistake.

We can go."

"This isn't a game, Colette. You understand?"

"I understand you're crazy. Willing to throw your new brother under the bus so I get punished. Let's just go."

Nicole hung up. She looked at her phone and said, "I can't save you, Colette. You have to save yourself."

"There's nothing to save."

Nicole looked up then. "No? This is all okay?"

Colette *hmphed* and brushed past Nicole on the way to the stairs.

Flynn watched for a moment, then said quietly, "Were you really calling the police?"

Nicole shook her head. "Nikita. Let's take my sister home."

Thirty-Five

It was crazy that Nikita looked like a supermodel even in the middle of the night.

Her face was makeup free but still striking in its beauty. Her hair was down around her shoulders and her dark purple robe belted high up under her breasts.

Those weren't real, Flynn knew from extensive experience. Boob jobs were the first work models had done.

But there was something in Nikita's bearing, in her eyes, in her movements, that said she would always be beautiful no matter how old she got and no matter what work she had done.

It was inside her.

And Flynn forgave his dad a little.

It was still gross, but Flynn got it. Got how this woman could make any man short-circuit, even if it was a memory.

He looked at Nicole, not seeing any of her mother in her at that moment.

No smiles, no laughter.

Just anger and worry, and Flynn reached for her hand so she didn't have to be angry and worried alone.

He squeezed gently, and Nikita said looking at their

joined hands, "Are you going to tell me his name now?"

Nicole looked like she was going to say no, so Flynn said it for her.

Nikita repeated it, stretching it out like she was tasting every letter, and Nicole said, "Mother. It's your other daughter, and *her* choice in men, you need to be worried about right now."

Nikita made a little sound of displeasure, then looked at Colette.

"Your brother, Colette? Really?"

"He's not *my* brother. I've never even met him, how was I supposed to know?"

Nicole said, "He's twenty-nine. Could that have stopped you?"

"Twenty-nine's too old, too? You're just never happy."

"I'm just not happy that you're apparently looking for a sugar daddy? No, I'm not."

"Gross. He's not that old. I just think teenage boys are boys and older guys are hot." Colette looked at Flynn. "Some of them."

Nikita looked at Flynn again, too, and Nicole's hand tightened around his. She said, "Some of them are *related*."

"I didn't know he was your brother!"

Colette's face flushed red and she spun around, nearly running to her bedroom.

They all watched, and Flynn thought there must be something in the Bissette bloodline. A bright neon light flashing around each of them, subconsciously shouting *look at me, look at me.*

Nicole closed her eyes a moment before Colette slammed her door shut but Flynn jumped.

Nikita was watching him and hardly let the echo of the shutting door fade before she said, "So, Ffllyynn, tell me about yourself."

Nicole tugged on his hand. "Let's go. We've delivered my prodigal sister to her uncaring *mother*."

Nikita said, still looking at Flynn, "I care. Don't make the mistake of thinking I don't."

"It's just so hard to see it," Nicole said, and Flynn had to disagree with her.

He could see it. Looking right at, and through, him.

Nikita said, "Give your sister a chance to apologize to you before you leave."

Nicole laughed, short and harsh, and Nikita said, "She's embarrassed that it was Scott she was making out with."

"Wha– How could you even know that?"

"Because, despite what you think, I know my daughter. And I know that she doesn't normally blush crimson when talking about men. She cares that he's your brother."

Nicole's mouth opened and then she just stood there, staring disbelieving at her mother.

Nikita pointed to Colette's door. "Don't talk. Just listen."

"You want me to just go in her room and say nothing?"

"Yes. Try it. You might enjoy the results."

Nicole looked torn, wanting to go after her sister and wanting to stay with Flynn, so he gave her a quick smile and let go of her hand.

"I'll be okay," he said, not believing it at all.

Nicole sighed, looked at Colette's door and then at her mother.

"Don't," she said, harshly, and Nikita put a hand to her chest as if to say, *Moi?*

Flynn thought the gesture looked very French.

Not French-American.

Nikita slid between the two of them, taking Flynn's arm and saying, "Would you like a drink while you wait, Ffllyynnnn?"

Nicole said, "If she offers you a syringe full of bleach, don't take it."

Flynn smiled at her, then was pulled away by Nikita.

He said truthfully, "I could do with a Red Bull, calm my nerves. Or a Coke, if you have it."

"I could do with a cigarette to calm mine. Daughters are so difficult. But I think we'll both be disappointed tonight."

She let go of his arm to push him into an oversized armchair, then left him alone while she headed to the kitchen.

He looked over his shoulder at Nicole, smiling again at her and getting an attempt at a smile in return before she turned and walked slowly after Colette.

He watched her knock quietly, then push the door in, and Flynn turned back around to stare at a pale cream sofa and a massive portrait hanging above it.

A younger Nikita lounging on a blanket in a field of grass, smiling out at the viewer. A baby laying in front of her, gumming ecstatically on her own hand, and an older girl sitting cross-legged at her mother's feet, her back to the viewer and watching the baby carefully.

Flynn knew it was Nicole, even though just a sliver of her face was visible, and he was studying it still when Nikita handed him a short, fat glass half-filled with Coke.

She sat down across from him on the sofa, pulling her feet up and tucking them under her robe.

She leaned forward, pulling open the door under the coffee table and pulling out a small machine. She wrapped tubing around her head and put a nose piece in her nose and said, "Oxygen. You have your substitute, and I have mine."

She flipped on the switch, a low humming sound coming to life, and sucked in a long puff of oxygen through her nose.

"It is a poor substitute. Dammit."

Flynn almost laughed, then remembered who he was talking to.

"But it makes me feel better, as I discovered a few years ago when oxygen bars were all the rage. I can trick myself, you see, into thinking that it's almost as good. More oxygen to the brain must feel better, don't you think?"

She laughed at herself, closing her eyes and leaning her head back and breathing in and out deeply.

Flynn drank his Coke, and then because his options were talk to Nikita, look at Nikita, or look at the portrait, he looked at the portrait.

After a long minute, she murmured, "It was a photo but I loved it so much, I had it painted."

Flynn flicked his eyes to her but she was still leaning with her head back and her eyes closed.

"Nicole hates it, of course, but it's so us. Me, only paying attention to the camera. Nicole hiding from it. Colette oblivious to it. Still true for all of us, or at least mostly true. I find that the older I get, the more I pay attention to. Like men who make my cautious, careful daughter a little less careful and cautious."

Flynn couldn't help it, he sat up a little at being called a man by Nikita.

But he didn't know what, or if, he was supposed to say anything and all he could think was, *Thanks?*

Maybe, *You're welcome?*

So he sipped his Coke and said, "Mm."

"I'd ask if you love my daughter but I already know you do."

Flynn choked on his next sip and Nikita chuckled.

"Don't take it personally. Any man she'd let get close enough to her would have to be in love with her."

And just like his dad, he made a face when he asked,

"Because she's beautiful and famous?"

"Because she's beautiful and famous. Because she has a vulnerability that she hates and tries to hide, and that makes men want to protect her. Because she wouldn't let any man get close to her unless *she* loved *him* and it would be impossible for any man not to love all of that in return."

Flynn's reply to that was: *gurgle gurgle cough gag hack thump thump.*

And when he could breathe again, he almost asked to share her oxygen.

He put his drink down on the coffee table, lucky and grateful he hadn't spilled it all over the chair, and looked up at the portrait.

At that sliver of Nicole, knowing that was all she would ever show anyone.

Just a sliver of herself. Hiding and protecting the rest of herself.

Away from all the eyes that had been watching her, judging her, since the day she was born.

Except she'd shown him so much more than a sliver. Maybe more than she'd shown anyone before.

Because. . .she loved him?

Tingle. Tingle.

In his toes. His fingertips.

The hair on the back of his neck stood up.

Maybe this wasn't crazy craziness.

Maybe this was love.

Body, heart, and soul.

Zap.

It felt about as good as he'd thought it would.

Like he'd never be the same again.

"Well," he said. "Well."

"Loving my daughter will not be easy, Ffllyynn."

He *did* know what to say to that and he was so flustered

by the thought that Nicole might actually– could she?– be in love with him, that he said it.

"No shit, Sherlock."

Nicole had already told him.

It's not going to be easy. I'm not easy.

If she'd been a normal girl, he would have realized sooner.

He would have been thinking about the future. Thinking about where they'd go from here.

But she wasn't normal.

She was Nicole *and* Nicole Bissette, and instead of realizing that maybe she was *it* in the comfort of his own home, here he was doing it while having some warped version of *the talk* with her mother.

He said, "And Nicole has already warned me."

Nikita smiled. "I have no doubt. But I will warn you again."

She opened her eyes and lifted her head and said, "You have an argument, there will be no complaining to a buddy over beer because it will find its way to the tabloids. Every vacation you take, you'll be followed, hunted, photographed. Any problems in your relationship will be whispered about and amplified until neither of you can remember the truth. Your parents will be staked out by neighbors who will be offered ludicrous amounts of money to alert the paps when she's visiting. Friends, and family, will become snitches and 'inside sources' because the money is just too good."

Nikita took another deep breath.

"And lord help us all if after love comes marriage. After marriage comes that baby carriage. *They* go crazy over wedding photos, pregnancy pics, baby shots. And Nicole will go crazy from the attention. More, when she will always want less."

Flynn already knew what that would look like, too.

Nicole hiding beside the AV cart, fear in her eyes. Hiding behind her desk, tears on her cheeks.

Nikita's eyes flicked over his shoulder and then she leaned forward.

"And above all that, every day of your life together, *you* will be judged. *You* will be found wanting. You will come up short and declared that you are not her equal. You are not *enough*. Why is she with you? And then, one day, she'll think it, too. You are not enough, and why is she with you? Because we all believe, eventually, what others tell us."

Flynn waited for her to continue and when she didn't, said, "They, and she, will be right, won't they?"

Nikita sat back and puffed in a breath, then opened her mouth to exhale as if she'd forgotten she wasn't really smoking.

"Maybe. But a relationship is destined to fail if it is not between equals. It will fail then, too, but for different reasons."

She sounded like she had experience with failed relationships.

Flynn looked up at the portrait again and said, "Okay. I accept."

Nikita's eyebrows pulled together a pinch. "You accept?"

Flynn nodded. "Of course we'll fail. Of course this crazy craziness won't last. Of course she'll realize one of these days that I am not enough and wonder why she's letting me be with her. I accept all of that. And I'll accept all of that for as long as she'll let me."

Nikita said, "Hmm," and Flynn didn't jump as Nicole leaned over his shoulder and pecked his cheek.

She murmured, "They're not right."

Flynn said, "They are, but I'd put up with any kind of

hell to be with you. And I'm not lying when I say your life sounds like hell."

She smiled at him, not looking like Nikita at all anymore, just looking like Nicole.

"Let's go home," she said. "I still want to finish watching Thor."

He smiled back, rising to follow her because he'd follow her anywhere.

"No, you don't."

Nicole glanced at her mother, not saying a word as they left. And Nikita just watched them go, puffing on her oxygen.

"Thank you for coming with me. And I'm sorry about my mother."

"She's not worse than mine, just different," Flynn said, and Nicole laughed in the darkness of her car.

"I don't know why you think so," she said and Flynn shrugged.

"Everybody thinks their parents are the worst. Except for those who don't, and something's just not right with them."

She reached for his hand and he could hear her smiling in the darkness. A streetlight would illuminate her face for a moment and then he could see it, too.

And he just watched.

Nicole in the dark. Nicole in the light.

Smiling at him, with him.

Showing him more than just a sliver.

He said, "I do love you. She was right about that."

And, *poof*, Nicole disappeared just like that. Not showing him anything anymore.

Her face froze and her hand slid from his.

And this is what he got for wanting more.

He'd realized what this was. And he'd wanted her to know, too.

Nicole looked towards him– not at him, just his general direction– and said, "Thank you, Flynn."

"Thank you?"

She nodded and he looked behind him in case he'd missed something. Anything.

He hadn't.

"Okay. Well. You're welcome."

He looked out the windscreen, at the lights now illuminating the hood.

In the dark. In the light. In the dark.

He waited a few, long silent minutes before saying, "I didn't think anything could be more awkward than your mother telling me I loved you. Guess it was me telling you."

He glanced at her turned-away face. "Was it something I wasn't supposed to say?"

Nicole said, "It's okay, I just don't know. . .how to reply."

"Well. That's what I said when your mother said it. Well."

"Well, then. Well?"

"It wasn't a question. It was, 'Well, then. Look at that. You're right.'"

Silence.

Stop.

No.

Not welcome.

Flynn looked out his side window.

They stopped at a red light and Nicole said softly, "We've only known each other *well* for a few months now. You can't really know me enough to love me."

His eyebrows flew up. "I can't know you enough to love you? Can I like you? I can want you?" He turned toward her again, saw the crack in her mask, and said, "Oh. You think I love Nicole Bissette."

"I am Nicole Bissette."

"No, you aren't. Okay, yes, you are. But that's not all you are. And that's not the part of you I love. She's got that crazy-bitch-I'm-resting face and I don't mind telling you that it's a little scary."

"Flynn–"

"But maybe you're right. Maybe it's too soon. I mean, if you don't think you might love me too, then I must think I love you because you're Nicole Bissette."

"You didn't say *I think I love you*. You said *I love you*."

He stared at her. "It loses a little something when you add the *I think* to the front of that statement."

"It would have made me feel better."

He continued to stare at her and she said, "*I think* it's safe to assume I have some issues. See how that makes it easier to swallow?"

"Easier to swallow. I see."

"Flynn. . ."

He took a deep breath. "Yes?"

She looked down at her hands gripping the steering wheel so tight it was going to break in two.

"Nothing to say," he said. "Can't even consider the idea that I might actually love you. Can't even let yourself wonder if you love me?"

He opened the door, in the middle of the night, on some random corner nowhere near his apartment.

"Well," he said, and he walked away.

Thirty-Six

The steering wheel cracked ominously under Nicole's hands and she oh-so-calmly took her hands off it.

And then she oh-so-gently locked the doors.

She watched Flynn walking away in her rearview mirror and she flinched when the car behind her honked its horn impatiently.

The light had turned green and Nicole didn't know what to do. Didn't want to leave Flynn, didn't want to go after him.

The other driver pulled around her, giving her the New York salute as he passed, and Nicole slowly angled her car over as far as she could and put on her hazard lights.

She watched Flynn wave down a taxi. Watched him get in.

Watched him drive off.

Nicole pulled back in to traffic, driving so slowly and so carefully that she pulled into the first parking spot she saw with relief.

She oh-so-gently picked up her phone and oh-so-calmly texted Gia.

Awake?

She closed her eyes and silently begged.

Please, please, please. Be awake.

Less than a minute later, her phone rang and Gia said hello with, "Did you know that they have the death penalty in Florida?"

Nicole said breathlessly, "I did not know that."

"I looked it up. And it may or may not be related, but lots of people die accidentally as well. On the beach, in the everglades, from too much beer."

"I'm sorry you want to kill your boss."

"Thank you. Why do you sound like you're talking through a straw?"

Nicole took a shallow breath.

"Because I think I'm hyperventilating."

"Put your head between your legs and take big breaths."

Nicole pushed her seat back so she could bend over, and Gia sing-songed, "Big breath in. Big breath out. One arm up. One arm down. One foot pointed. One foot flexed. One eye open. One eye closed. One cheek clenched. One cheek loose."

Nicole opened both eyes and sat up. "Are you just making this up?"

"Worked didn't it? Why were you having a panic attack?"

"I've had a really rough couple of hours."

"Story time! Let me get comfortable. . . Okay, go."

Nicole didn't go. She just sat there, not knowing what to say and where to start. Not even to someone who knew her and loved her and wouldn't be at all surprised that *she had issues*.

Gia waited a beat, then said, "Just start at the beginning."

So Nicole started at the beginning of the end.

"Scott called me from a club because he'd been making out with Colette."

And wasn't it both funny and sad that the knot Nicole hadn't realized was squeezing her stomach and chest loosened when she could focus on Scott and Colette and not Flynn.

Gia said, "Wait, Victoria's Scott? Your brother, Scott?"

"Yes."

"Well, that's... I'm trying to work it out... Are they blood related in any way?"

"No."

"Okay. So the ick factor is just that you're related to both of them and it's not actually illegal?"

"It's illegal. She's seventeen." Nicole took another, slightly bigger, breath. "She says they didn't, you know, though. So not illegal, I guess."

"Isn't her birthday coming up, too?"

"Thank you. You're really helping me get through this."

Gia laughed. "Sorry. You're right. Next month, when she's still your sister and he's still your brother and the age difference is no longer illegal but still disturbingly large, their relationship will still be icky. This is all Nonna's fault."

Nicole could normally follow along the jumps Gia made with her logic, but this escaped her.

"How is this your grandmother's fault? If anything, it's still my mother's. Should have told us all years ago."

Gia cackled in an old witch's voice, "*Your brother will fall in love with your sister, he will!* Doesn't that sound like a curse that would accompany the evil eye?"

Nicole blinked. Then her shoulders started to shake. And then the laughter poured from her along with a few lonely tears.

She found a tissue in her purse, wiping her eyes and her

nose and saying, "Okay, that helped. They don't have a relationship, they aren't in love with each other. It was just an accidental hookup at a club. It's not like they're going to even see each other again."

And while Nicole hated to admit her mother could be right about anything, Colette *had* been embarrassed that Scott was her brother.

Nicole had gone into her room, not saying a word, and Colette hadn't said anything either. Just looked at herself in her vanity mirror until she'd cried out, *He's your brother!*

Yeah.

I know you think I have daddy issues but this is weird right here! Did I know? How could I have known?

I didn't know. Victoria almost married him and I didn't know.

Really?

Nicole had nodded and Colette had sniffed.

I was attracted to my sister's brother. Like, seriously. I took one look at him and wanted him. I don't know what that says about me but I'm pretty sure it's not good!

Nicole had kept her face carefully blank and said, *We don't look anything alike.*

No, that's true. You're a mini-Nikita. Anyone could have been your father, she'd said and then jumped from her chair. *Maybe he's* not *your brother!*

They did a blood test.

Colette had deflated again and then said in a small, sad voice, *Do you think it was, like, unconscious?*

And Nicole had hugged her and petted her hair.

No. Scott doesn't look anything like me. He's handsome and has perfect hair. He wears a TAG Heuer and $500 pants. He's catnip to your inner kitten.

He really is. I just wanted to rub myself all over him.

Please, stop.

Colette had squeezed her so tight and whispered, *Are you mad at me?*

Yes, I'm mad at you. Mad that you went to that club, mad that you were doing who knows what drugs. Mad that you'd made out with some random dude who was twelve years older than you. I'm not mad that it turned out to be Scott.

Okay, good. All that other stuff you were already mad at me for anyway. I'm glad it's not anything new. Glad it's not because I'm weird and messed up.

Gia said, "You sure they're not going to see each other again?"

"Colette is freaking out about it still. Scott looked like he wanted to drown himself in the nearest toilet. If he gets over it too quickly. . . I'll do something. I don't know."

"You can sick Victoria on him."

Because adding another messed-up relationship to the mix would surely make everything all better.

Nicole asked reluctantly, "Have you talked to her?"

"Yes. She'll get over it."

Nicole didn't know about that.

"Don't let her be alone right now, okay?"

"You can call her, you know."

"I'm complicated. He's my brother now and let me tell you something, it complicates things!"

"So you're just going to let her get over it before you talk to her again? Victoria?"

Nicole smiled a little. "No. I'll call her. When I think she should be over it."

"I'll let you wait until *I* think she should be over it."

"Okay."

"Okay. Now what else happened tonight because it sounds like disaster was averted re: Scott and Colette."

And Nicole just blurted it out because she didn't think she could get it out any other way.

"Flynn told me he loves me."

Gia gasped. "*Awwww.*"

"I told him he didn't."

Gia sucked in a breath. "*Ayyyyy*. This was a bad time to move away."

"There was never going to be a good time."

"Probably true. Was he naked when he told you? It's pretty common knowledge that's a bad time to do it and you could make the whole conversation his fault."

"No. We'd just come from dropping Colette home and he just said, 'I love you,' like. . . like. . . like he just wanted me to know."

Gia waited.

Nicole whispered, "I told him thank you."

"Okay, I can hear your voice closing up again. Put your head back between your knees and big breath in. Big breath out. One hand open. Smack your self."

"Oh, just stop it. I know it was bad. I can't think of anything worse I could have said."

"Die rebel scum?"

Nicole leaned her seat all the way back and put her arm over her eyes.

"What am I going to do?"

"Go watch *Notting Hill*."

Nicole pulled her arm from her eyes.

"Huh?"

"Go watch it. I'll wait."

Gia hung up.

Nicole called her right back.

"I'm in crisis mode here!"

"I know. Thus the romantic comedy featuring the adorable Hugh Grant when he was adorable and not too old to be in a romantic comedy." Gia took a breath. "You've tried sugar, it was an epic fail. Try this. And don't call me back until you've watched it."

Gia hung up again and Nicole put her phone away.

She put her seat back up.

And then, because she had no friends left, and sugar was a definite fail, she went home and found *Notting Hill* online and watched it.

A couple hours later, Nicole called Gia back, not caring whether she was awake or not.

Gia answered, groggy but lucid, with, "Did you really watch it or did you just wait long enough for me to think you watched it?"

"I really watched it."

"And?"

"And what?"

"*Thank you, Gia. Now I know exactly what to do.*"

Nicole said, "First of all, my life is not a movie."

"Mm-hm."

"And second of all, the answers to Life, the Universe and Everything are not in a fifteen-year-old rom-com featuring the adorable Hugh Grant."

Adorable. . .

Were men allowed to be adorable in real life? Sweet?

Selfless and kind?

Were they allowed to be support staff? Play second fiddle?

Gia sighed. "Go watch it again. I'll wait."

"Don't hang up–"

Nicole shook her head at the dial tone and put her phone away, wondering what kind of life you had to live to actually believe in happy-ending, fairy-tale love.

She was awoken a few hours later by the incessant ringing of her phone and was a lot more groggy and a lot less lucid than her friend when Gia said, "Did you watch it again?"

"I decided to sleep instead."

"What happened to crisis mode?"

"I think five a.m. happened to crisis mode."

"Then let me remind you. A wonderfully normal man told you he loved you and you said... say it with me now... thank you!"

Nicole closed her eyes, wanting to hide under her covers forever.

Gia said, "Now then. What did you learn from Notting Hill?"

"Nothing."

"Nope. You learned that a regular Joe Schmoe *can* fall in love with a goddess. You learned that a goddess *can* fall in love with a regular Joe Schmoe. Have you?"

"What?"

"Fallen in love with your regular Joe Schmoe?"

"Of course not," Nicole said without thinking.

"Because..."

"I don't know what love is supposed to look like. I've never seen it before."

"Bullhonky. You have. And even if that was really true, you don't have to have seen it before to know what love looks like."

"Gia, this is *real life*."

"Nicole, do you love Flynn? Don't think about it, don't worry about it. Just answer me. Do you love Flynn?"

"Yes! I love him! Maybe! It doesn't matter!"

"It matters. Go say it back to him. Tell him you're sorry and you love him. Tell him you maybe love him. Tell him he matters."

Nicole hung her head. "I can't. I'm afraid."

So afraid, even Gia's grandmother could see it.

Your beauty has cut too many times and you are afraid of it.

Afraid of her own beauty, afraid of others, afraid of having a life.

Gia said, "That's because this is real life and love is scary. Love means there is something, someone, out there that you care about more than yourself. That's pretty scary."

It was terrifying, and Nicole said, "It won't last."

"It might. Are you afraid it will or are you afraid it won't?"

"Yes."

Gia crooned in the back of her throat and said, "Here. This is me stroking your nice, soft, *straight* hair. This is me holding you and telling you that I love you. And this is me telling you that you love me, and Victoria, and Colette, already. You maybe love Scott, and maybe love Nikita. And adding one more love or even one more maybe love to your life is something good. Adding one more person who will love you in return, adding one more person who will have your back when you need it most, is worth the fear."

Nicole choked back a sob. She could feel it, an invisible hand tenderly stroking her hair and she said, "I told him *thank you.*"

Gia chuckled. "Oh, yeah, you're going to have to grovel. No doubt about that."

"Will he even forgive me?"

"Of course he will. Love forgives. You called me plus-sized and I forgave you, remember?"

Nicole smiled through the tears. "Really having a hard time forgetting."

"That's because love also likes to repeatedly remind you

of your mistakes."

"Someday I'd like to meet your family in person."

"Oh, they'd like that! You should come visit. You can help me hide my boss's body."

Thirty-Seven

It was freezing.

The wind was blowing and the clouds were swirling and Nicole could feel the air getting heavier, wetter.

A storm was coming, and when Flynn opened his parent's front door, Nicole thought she'd rather stay outside with it than go in with him.

He said, "I didn't think you were coming."

"I needed to talk to you. I want to talk to you."

He waved her inside and she didn't move. She handed him a white apparel gift box.

"I made it for you," she said and he pulled the lid off, dug through the tissue paper. He pulled out a gray lightweight wool suit jacket.

"You made me a suit?"

She nodded. "I wanted you to have a suit you loved. So you don't have to wear one you hate. So you know how it feels when you love what you wear."

"That's very important to you, I know," he said, smiling slightly, and she whispered, "Look good, feel good. I've been working on it for a while."

He put it back in the box and she said, "Um, there's

more to it," and she reached for the jacket, pulling it back out.

She opened it up, turning it inside out to show the half of a stylized black and gray S on each side, and then closed it to show what it would look like when it was buttoned.

"I know, it's backwards. He takes off the suit. But I thought, when you buttoned it up, you would feel it. And it would still be on your chest so. . ."

He looked at her. "You made me a Superman suit?"

He dropped the box, pulling the jacket from her fingers and up his arms and buttoning it up. His shoulders went back and his chest went out and he said, "Okay, I get it. I'd pay $3000 for this."

"It doesn't cost that much. Only a second chance. Please, and I'm sorry, and I didn't mean thank you."

"What did you mean?"

She'd meant love. Maybe love.

She said, "It never ends well for a man in love with a Bissette."

Breath rushed past his lips in a half laugh. "I noticed."

"It doesn't end well for the Bissette, either."

Flynn carefully shoved his hands in the jacket pockets.

"So you're never going to try? Just going to keep your heart locked up?"

Nicole squeezed her hands into fists.

"I was telling you that I'm in love with you. Maybe."

Flynn blinked and the silence lengthened.

Nicole finally said, "I love you. I *think* I love you. I'm not a hundred percent sure because I've never been in love before. No one's ever loved me before. *Me.*" She put her hands to her chest, thumping lightly. "Men have said those words before and I've never believed them. And I'm sorry that I didn't believe you when you said it. Not at first."

"You believe me now?"

She wanted to say yes. Wanted to tell him she did.

But she told him the truth instead.

"I don't know. But I *want* to believe. I want to believe that if you don't really– not quite– love me yet, that maybe you could. Maybe you will."

He waited for more but that was all she had. She *wanted* to believe him, wanted it so badly that she'd come here even when she'd known it would end like this.

He said, "Not going to lie. This, I hate."

"Me, you mean."

He waved his hands between them. "*This*. This *maybe*. This *I think*."

"I've given all I can give right now, Flynn."

"And I thought it would be enough. I thought I would give anything to be with you. Go through any kind of hell but now. . . what's going to happen when I want more? Because I keep wanting more from you, Nicole, and what's going to happen when I want everything? When I want your whole heart and your whole life. When I want our future and our children, when I want *us* and no more me and you? If I'm going to have to walk through hell, I want to know you'll be there with me the whole time, and now I'm afraid you won't be."

"I'm always afraid. I can't stop worrying," she said, taking a step closer to him. Wanting to give him all of her truth, even if it wouldn't be enough. "Except when I'm with you. You're my closet. My refuge. When I'm with you, I feel safe." Nicole opened her arms, kept her eyes wide open, and opera-ed, "*Sanctuary!*"

Flynn didn't smile. He looked down.

"See, I want to give you that. I love you, and I'd give you anything I could. I just. . . I need a sanctuary, too." He looked up, meeting her eyes sadly. "I didn't know that I wouldn't want to do this with you. Right up until this moment, I just didn't know."

Nicole whispered, "Can't know what you don't know until you know it," and felt the first fat, cold raindrops fall from the sky.

Flynn closed the door behind him softly, took his new Superman jacket off gently, and then fell limply onto the couch.

His mom said, "Where's Nicole?"

"Went home."

Lisa pulled back the curtain and said, "She's just standing out there in the rain. She's going to catch her death."

She waited for Flynn to get up and when he didn't, huffed loudly and went outside herself.

Flynn almost got up to look out the window, but she came hurrying back in a moment later, alone and shaking water from her arms.

"She won't come in. Mike!"

Mike poked his head from the kitchen where he'd been hiding since Nicole had first knocked on the door.

"What do you want me to do about it?"

"Get her to come inside!"

Mike looked at his wife, then his son still sitting lifelessly on the couch. He went to the door, opening it to look at Nicole.

He shut it.

"Mike!"

"What do you want me to do, Lisa? Carry her inside fireman-style?"

He went back to the kitchen, Lisa following behind him, whispering furiously.

Flynn fingered the material of his new suit, looked at

the inside of the two sides but didn't put them together.

She'd made him a suit. And he would bet it looked great, felt amazing.

He'd never be able to wear it, not without thinking of her.

His dad sat down next to him and passed him a beer and a bag of chips.

"So."

"So."

Mike grabbed the remote, turning on the TV and turning the volume way down. "Guess that's over."

"Guess so."

"Probably for the best."

"Thanks, Dad."

"You know. Just. She's Nicole Bissette."

Flynn sipped, and took a deep breath, and ate a chip.

Then he said, "No, she's not. Nicole Bissette is some kind of character. . . some kind of caricature. Nicole is more than that."

"Oh?"

"She's careful and cautious but she keeps standing back up. She wants to hide but she doesn't. She looks beautiful but she wants others to *feel* it. She makes me a Superman suit but won't tell me she loves me without a maybe. She's just standing out there in the rain and I don't know what she wants from me!"

Mike grabbed a handful of chips. "Women. Can't get away from that, son."

A loud thump from the kitchen made Mike jump and he cleared his throat. "But I mean, what would we do without them?"

Flynn took another deep breath, another sip. "Why is Mom hiding around the corner while we're having this little heart-to-heart?"

"She said I had to do it. And I say this as your father, Flynn, but a man does what his woman wants him to. Even when, *especially when*, he doesn't know exactly what that is."

"Why can't they just tell us what they want?

Lisa said loudly, "Oh, we *try*. It just never works."

"Mom, come on out."

Lisa came around the corner, saying, "Nicole probably told you what she wanted, you just weren't listening."

Had she told him? All Flynn had heard was maybe.

Maybe she loved him.

Maybe she believed he loved her.

"Nope." Flynn shook his head. "I got nothing."

Mike glanced at Lisa. "Sometimes you've got to read between the lines," he said and Lisa sighed.

"She needs you to be her sanctuary. She sang it to you!"

Mike and Flynn considered this, and Flynn said, "But I need that, too. Don't I?"

Mike said, "She's already given you what you need," and Lisa and Flynn both looked at him.

"You needed a woman you'd bring home to me and your mom. A woman who'd steal your heart and then offer it back to you. A woman who'd make you smile and laugh and come alive. A woman who'd make you feel like Superman and make you a damn suit to go with it. A woman who–"

"All right. Okay. I get it."

"Don't think you do. You're still here. She's already given you what all men need. A woman who thinks they're a ten, 'cause none of us are. And when you find that woman, you give her whatever you think she wants from you. You're going to be wrong; give it to her anyway."

"Nicole doesn't think I'm a ten."

"The woman is standing on the front lawn in the

pouring rain. She sang to you. She thinks you're a ten. And my guess is she's trying to give you all she can. Trying to give you what she thinks you want. She's going to be wrong. Take it from her anyway."

Flynn put his beer down and went to the window, looking at Nicole standing in the pouring rain.

Waiting. For what exactly, Flynn didn't know.

But still waiting.

He heard his dad say softly, "Is that what you wanted?"

He heard the smile in his mom's voice. "No. But it was still pretty good."

"There's just no pleasing you women."

There was a pause before she said, "But we really like it when you try," and Flynn was forced out the door before he started hearing kissy noises.

He stopped on the porch, shutting the door behind him, and stared at Nicole.

Soaking wet and shivering and waiting for him to try again, and Flynn ran to her.

He shouted over the storm, "What do you want, Nicole? From me? What's my best answer when you say you maybe love me?"

"Say you maybe love me back! Until I'm not afraid. Until I love you, no maybe."

He wrapped his arms around her, feeling her shaking. "Will you tell me when you're sure? When there's no maybe?"

"Yes."

"No, I mean really tell me. No hints, just tell me outright. Don't make me guess, don't make me get it wrong."

"I will."

He put his lips against hers. "Well. I accept. I'll wait."

She put her arms around his neck, hiding her face

against his cheek and saying, "I never wanted to believe before. Maybe I do love you."

Flynn pulled back. "Is this me now? My turn?"

She nodded, smiling, and Flynn said, "Maybe I love you, too."

* * *

Printed in Great Britain
by Amazon